PURE INSTINCT

Ellen Fletcher

A KISMET™ Romance

METEOR PUBLISHING CORPORATION
Bensalem, Pennsylvania

First Printing June 1992.

ISBN: 1-56597-010-1

Printed in the United States of America.

To Kate Duffy, Terri Register and everyone at Meteor who made getting this novel into publication as much fun as writing it. And especially to Catherine Carpenter. The opportunity to work with you has been KISMET.

ELLEN FLETCHER

Ellen Fletcher began writing seriously at age fifteen when she created, wrote and produced a children's radio program, Fun 'n Fancy, that aired five days a week. Since then, she's done commercial art, advertising design, and copywriting. She now writes fiction full time. A North Carolina native, she lives with her husband, a daughter, and five cats—two of whom are Charlie and Brigette who helped write this novel.

ONE

"Smile, Amie. Channel Three's Live Eye is focused directly at you."

Amie Phillips flashed a smile as dazzling as her beauty, then turned to her escort, Dr. Thomas Delahunt, her best friend's husband. "That's a stroke of luck," Amie said. "Now we'll be on the late news and everybody will know we were here doing our civic duty. Why can't we leave now?"

She wasn't surprised when Tom ignored her question, taking her arm when someone jostled her.

"Pardon me."

Amie turned to see the stranger who'd bumped into her, then wished she hadn't when their eyes met. In that instant she felt as if he'd captured her.

Seized by a strange fascination she was at a loss to understand, Amie stared at the back of the tall, broad-shouldered man. His hand cupped the elbow of a slender brunette who was wearing a red silk organza Armani. Amie remembered seeing it at a boutique when she was shopping for her own gown and it had caught her eye, even then. She also remembered gagging when she saw the price tag. Now, however, it was more than the brunette or the dress she was wearing that held Amie's attention.

"Would you look at that!" she muttered to Tom. "I'm surprised he isn't wearing boots with spurs."

In a room filled with formally dressed people, a wool shearling jacket of muted earth tones was draped over the man's shoulder. Beneath it was a burgundy Western-style bib shirt and brown double-pleated slacks. Weird for the occasion. Thick brown hair dared to curl at the nape of his neck, and Amie thought he tilted his head rather arrogantly.

"Know him?" Tom asked with a big grin.

In the same instant, her captor turned to look back at her. For a heartbeat they stared at each other. Amie couldn't resist smiling, but she was not prepared for his outrageous response. He grinned . . . and winked. *Winked.*

"Never seen him before," she said. *Except in my dreams.* Even as she spoke, she was aware of an uncanny recognition she felt somewhere deep inside her. It made her shiver as she turned back to Tom, determined to push the image of penetrating blue eyes from her mind.

The orchestra struck up a slow number and Amie turned to Tom. "There are so many people here, no one would have noticed if I'd stayed home with a good book."

Tom still gaped after the couple and Amie guessed it was not the red dress that held his attention either, but rather the brunette in it. "Aren't you going to tell me who they are?" Amie asked. "That is, if you can tear your gaze from that red dress."

Tom grinned sheepishly. "The guy's Buck Cameron, one of *the* Camerons. The knockout with him is Celia Stockton, the lady judge." He gave Amie a mock little bow. "But she can't hold a candle to you, your highness. The thing is, if I drool over you, you'll punch me or kick me in the shins."

"Why, I wouldn't do that," Amie teased. "I'd let Millie do it for me."

She didn't have to ask who the Camerons were. They weren't simply pillars of the community, but more like its foundation. There was hardly a city in the South that didn't boast one or more Cameron Department Store. And everyone knew Buck Cameron was crazy—not crazy as in lunatic, but as in oddball, screwball, wild, and eccentric. No wonder he'd been able to confound her with no more than a look.

"I've heard he keeps his Christmas tree up the year 'round," she said, wishing now for a longer look at him.

Tom chuckled. "Yeah, I've heard the same thing. He also stalks women and wild animals. I hear his favorite hunting ground is Peru."

"So, what's Celia Stockton doing with him? You'd think a lady judge would be more cautious."

"I guess she thinks he's worth a risk. Buck's about thirty-six and already a multi-millionaire. The old man was in the state legislature so long he became a fixture, and the eldest son, Wicket, is one of your congressional representatives. With their money and political clout, they just about control this city, if not the whole state."

"Ummm. That takes care of the father and the eldest son," Amie mused. "I take it this one is the black sheep?"

"Don't let Buck fool you. He's chief executive officer of the family business. Eccentric, but a damned likable guy. For my money, he's the best of the lot."

"For your money, but not for mine," Amie said emphatically. "I don't understand people who can kill an animal, wild or not. It's barbaric."

"Hey, you don't see me with a gun, do you? Come on. Let's find our places at the table, and then I'll give you the thrill of your life. I'll let you dance with me."

"That's big of you." Amie tried not to think about Buck Cameron. Refocusing her thoughts, she wondered for the umpteenth time how she'd let Millie talk her into taking her place at this shindig. She was not of a mind to rub shoulders with the likes of Buck Cameron. Of all the times for Millie to get the flu!

The truth was, Amie didn't feel so great herself. Exhausted from long hours at work, she wondered if she hadn't caught Millie's virus. She'd almost fallen asleep in the shower tonight, and it was an effort to dress and do her makeup so Tom wouldn't see how tired she was. Once she'd agreed to come, she wanted to look good for him for Millie's sake. Now she wished she were home in bed. Not only was she tired; she'd never enjoyed being with so many people at one time.

Sighing, she thought about her *investment,* as Millie referred to the new gown she'd talked her into buying. She knew she'd be thinking about if for some time hence—every time her credit card statement came.

"Are you listening to me, Amie?"

"What?" She looked quickly up at Tom. "Of course, I am. What were you saying?"

"That . . .

Amie laughed. "I heard you, Tom. You said you were going to give me a thrill. I could use one about now."

"Well, here's the table." Tom stopped at a lavishly decorated table reserved for five-hundred-dollar patrons. The band struck up and Amie decided to try her luck one more time. "Honest, Tom. All the hospital bigwigs have already seen that you're here. Can't I talk you into going home, now that you've met your social obligation?"

"Not on your life. Here I am, ready to show you what a great dancer I am and you're still trying to renege on me."

"I'm trying to help you save face. I've worked twelve hours a day for the past week," she admitted, "and I feel like a zombie. What'll you do if I pass out in your arms?"

"Not to worry. There's a doctor in the house."

Amie laughed at Tom's tired witticism and wondered how she was going to make it through the evening. She'd been out very little since she moved to Charlotte. And, of course, Millie used that as part of her argument to persuade her to attend the Heart Ball with Tom. Millie didn't seem to understand that she was not ready to be part of the social scene. Not yet. For the time being, her work was more than enough. Finding homes for the homeless was not an easy job. Sometimes she wondered if she'd taken on more than she could handle.

"Come on, Amie." Tom gave her an admiring look as he held out his hand. "Some women have a knockout face and some have a great body. When you have both, you have an obligation to show it off."

Amie laughed and punched him. "Now I know how you caught Millie. You lied through your teeth and she bought it."

"Modesty . . ."

". . . becomes me. Yeah, I know." She laid her purse on the table in front of her place card—a small, red ceramic heart on which her name was written in script—and followed Tom onto the dance floor.

"Who knows," Tom said, "we may bump into just the person who'll come to your aid the next time you need a big donation for Crisis House."

After an oldie but goodie from the big band and a current release by a local group she liked better, the mistress of ceremonies announced dinner would be served at the end of the next dance. Then both groups of musicians played together—something with hearts in the title—and Amie felt dead on her feet by the time Tom escorted her back to their table. He pulled back her chair and she slid into it and out of her high-heeled sandals.

The first thing she noticed was that Buck Cameron and Celia Stockton were sitting to her right. She glanced toward them when she heard Buck laugh, but neither he nor his date seemed to notice her. His jacket was draped over the back of his chair, and in his burgundy shirt he was the only man present who didn't resemble a ruffled penguin. She stared curiously at his sharp profile.

The little she could see of him from that angle only made her want to see more. Deeply tanned, his complexion seemed too smooth, especially for an outdoorsman. The creases at the corner of his mouth suggested he must smile often. She wished he'd turn around so she could see his eyes again.

"Amie?"

She looked at Tom, hoping he hadn't seen her staring at Buck Cameron, but apparently she'd been more obvious than she'd realized.

"Better watch out for that one," Tom whispered with a mischievous grin. "Just because I said he's likable doesn't mean he's safe. His reputation with women spans oceans and leaps tall mountains."

"Another Joe Cannon, huh?" Amie grunted, reminded of the relationship she'd ended just before moving to Charlotte.

"Even worse," Tom warned.

A waiter placed their dinner before them and for the next few minutes Amie was too busy eating to ask questions.

"You haven't eaten all week?" Tom teased.

"At five hundred dollars a plate, surely you don't expect me to leave anything." When the last bite of dessert was gone, Amie sighed contentedly and leaned back in her chair while Tom still nibbled at the sinful chocolate concoction the waiter had brought them. One of the bands had begun to play and many couples were already dancing.

"You shouldn't eat so fast," Tom chided. "I have the feeling it's a habit you've picked up since you've been in Charlotte. Millie tells me she can't get you away from work long enough to have lunch with her."

"Millie's a tattletale," Amie said with a smile.

"She's worried about you."

Before she could explain to Tom that her work was her salvation, she felt a hand on her shoulder. "Excuse me, Amie," the deep voice said.

Slowly she turned her head to look into the most riveting blue eyes she'd ever seen. A whimsical little smile tilted the corners of her soft, full lips.

"I believe this next dance is ours." Buck slid her chair backward. Pure instinct made her slip her feet into her sandals and lay her hand into his outstretched palm. Holding her gaze, Buck closed his hand tightly around hers.

Head on, the man was formidable. More than six feet of power and masculinity swept her senses, and his blue eyes had the same effect on her as the first time they ensnared her. While his mouth hinted at a smile, Amie suspected those sensuous lips could also be cruel. Yes, he belongs in a jungle, all right, she thought, wondering if it were her imagination or if she'd caught a scent of wildness about him. Something resembling a shudder chased through her. She took a deep breath, then almost laughed aloud at the only thought her mind could conjure. *Never let them see you sweat.*

"I'm looking forward to this." Buck's voice was smooth as dark honey and when he drew her into his arms an unbidden excitement took hold of her. For an instant, she thought she'd lost it. Never had she been so aware of a man's sexual magnetism. She resented the feeling, but knew nothing could keep her from dancing with him.

"How do you know my name?" she asked, struggling to regain her composure as they glided across the polished floor.

"Even I can read," he said with amusement, drawing her so close she could barely breathe. Even with four-inch heels, her chin came barely to his shoulder, but he tilted his head slightly to the side so their cheeks touched.

"Oh," she murmured, remembering the place cards. But not for long. Practical details were nothing compared to the sensation of being held in his arms.

He'd ignored her all through dinner, but now he was holding her as if he never intended to let her go. And for now, that suited her just fine.

They moved across the floor as if they'd been dancing together for years. Of course, how could they miss when they were melded into one? Through the thin white silk of her gown she could feel the hard muscles of his thighs. There was barely an inch of him she couldn't feel, and she was keenly aware of the sinewy body that guided her through the most intricate steps.

"I'm glad you were hungry," she heard Buck say.

"You're *what?*"

He laughed softly and Amie wondered if the ripples cascading down her back were vibrations from his laughter or something inside her.

"I like a woman with a healthy appetite. And I've been anxious to check out your moves. With a body like yours . . ."

"My *what?*"

Again he chuckled, and when he whirled her across the floor, she noticed that other dancers good naturedly made way for them. She imagined he was used to such deference and she couldn't understand why it didn't make her angry.

"My instincts are pretty good," he said. "When I first saw you, I knew our rhythms were in sync. That doesn't happen very often, you know."

"And you think one dance can verify that? You must put a lot of faith in your instincts."

"The dance is just a prelude," he said too smoothly, entirely too seductively, and with an authority that said his intention was absolute.

Amie's heartbeat quickened and she missed a step. *Get hold of yourself, Amie Phillips.* Any woman who can't recognize a well-practiced line has to be more foolish than naive. *So, why are your knees coming unhinged?*

This was simply not rational. She didn't want to be excited by a man . . . any man . . . and especially not this one. From what Tom had said, Buck Cameron was not only a womanizer. He hunted wild things. She was not ready to be shot down again.

His breath was warm against her cheek when he lowered his head. "About twenty feet from here there's a door that leads to an exit. Are you game?"

"You *are* crazy!" Amie stopped dancing and pushed against him. "You don't know me from Adam."

"Eve." He laughed rustily as he pulled her back against him. "And I must admit, this gown you're wearing is quite a fig leaf."

She thought she'd choke on her own vivid imagination. She could just see Buck Cameron's rock-hard body hidden by only a fig leaf. Maybe with the wind blowing?

"Of course," he added, "even in a gunnysack, it would be hard to miss you, darlin'. And you must know who I am because you were staring at me all through dinner."

"I was *not* staring." In a much lower voice she added, "Not all through dinner."

His voice filled with amusement. "Yes, you were," he insisted. "Not that I minded. In fact, I rather liked it. But I can tell by the way you said I was crazy that you're already prejudiced. So, you have to know my name."

"Anybody who comes to something like this dressed the way you are has to be crazy, fella."

He held his head back and laughed so loudly Amie

was certain every single person in the ballroom was staring at them. She tightened her hand on his shoulder. "When you work for city government, as I do," she muttered, "you have to watch your reputation. Now dance, dammit."

"I'm sorry, Amie," he said, trying to swallow his laughter. He twirled her toward the door he had mentioned. "You're such a delight, I forgot myself."

"You also forgot the direction back to our table."

"I heard you tell Tom that you wanted to leave. I knew then that you were a woman after my own heart."

His heart? Never. But this body . . . "Tom?"

"Your escort, remember?"

Of course, she remembered. What did he think? That she was totally and completely mesmerized by his, uh, charms?

"He's married, isn't he? To Millie Adkins?"

"He and Millie are my best friends."

"Ah, I see," said Buck, nodding his head in a way that moved his chin against the top of her head. "Well, I happen to know that Tom's a decent guy. He'll be happy to take Celia home when he realizes we've left."

She'd begun to feel a bit dizzy with that last twirl. Later, she realized it must have been a combination of the heat in the overly crowded room, the rich food, and the long hours she'd been working—to say nothing of Millie's virus that she was afraid was taking hold of her. The room began to whirl about her, distorted strains of music reached her ears, and tiny sparks of white light danced before her eyes.

"You'll have to forgive me," she said to Buck. "I have to go back to the table because I don't feel very well."

Buck put a little distance between them so he could see her face. It was too much to hope that she'd been overcome by his charms. "You're serious," he said anxiously. Beads of perspiration sparkled on her forehead and the blush on her high cheekbones was bright against the paleness of her skin. He brushed back the cloud of hair that framed her face. Her eyes seemed unfocused.

"It's a long way back to the table," he said with concern. "Anyway, you probably need some fresh air. Think you can make it to the door?"

She thought about Tom, but knew it would be impossible to find him in the sea of people undulating around them. Not knowing what else to do, she nodded her head and forced a sickly smile, grateful for the strong arm that supported her.

Buck pushed open a heavy door that led onto a wide stone veranda overlooking a golf course. Though the rush of cold, fresh air buoyed her, she still felt dizzy. "I'm so sorry," she apologized, her voice barely audible. "A chair . . ."

He looked in vain for a place to sit, then mumbled an obscenity. Even in her woozy state, Amie was conscious of the ease with which he suddenly lifted her into his arms. "I'll hold you," he said, folding her close.

"No . . ." She pushed ineffectively against one of his shoulders only to discover she had neither the strength nor the will to object forcibly.

"Be still, Amie. I thought the cold air would make you feel better, but I'm not sure now that it's a good idea. It's chilly for you out here without a wrap. My body heat should keep you warm for a few minutes, though." To say nothing about the rise in his own temperature. He looked at the soft bundle that lay so close to his heart. The light of the moon made a halo about her face and she didn't appear so pale now, though he could discern shadowed circles beneath her eyes. On Amie, even they looked good. With her finely sculpted cheekbones, the pale shadows gave her beauty an ethereal quality.

She didn't seem the type to dissipate her strength. But hell, what did he know about her except what his instincts told him?

Amie saw that he was watching her curiously. "I feel much better already," she murmured, mortified by her predicament. "I think it's safe to go back inside."

"Don't squirm," he said, refusing to put her down. "I saw how you looked in there, and the shadows beneath your eyes mean something. The way you put your dinner away, I can't believe you're one of those women who starves herself, so you must be coming down with something . . . the flu, maybe. It's going around, you know."

Buck's embrace was having a very undesired effect. Buck Cameron was an unnerving man—a fact that was compounded by being so close to him. If she hadn't been innoculated against his type, she might easily fall prey to his macho strength, the knowing blue eyes, the teasing mouth that moved so sensuously. Thank heaven, she *was* immune. But despite the fact that she still had trouble focusing her eyes, she thought to free herself.

"I told you to stop squirming," he warned with a wicked flash of his eyes. "It isn't my nature to take advantage of a woman not up to defending herself, but if you keep this up I won't be responsible for the consequences."

"Then put me down!"

Too quickly, she was on her feet. She hadn't meant to sound so adamant, but neither had she intended to find herself swept off her feet, literally, by Buck Cameron.

"Let's see how well you can maneuver," he said.

"I'm sorry about this," she said again. "I'm not sure what hit me, but thanks for the rescue."

"You're still not too steady," Buck observed. "Best let Tom check you over tomorrow." He put his arm around her shoulders. "I hope you're not chilled," he said, watching her face closely. He imagined she wouldn't admit she was cold if she turned to ice. Before holding her, he hadn't been so keenly aware of the loveliness of the woman beside him. Nor could he forget how she'd felt when, just for a moment, she'd relaxed against him. He wished he could see beyond the surface beauty. For the first time in a long time, he wanted to know more about a woman than how long it would take him to get her into the sack.

"No, I'm fine. Really," Amie insisted, "the cold air was exactly what I needed. Thanks for saving me from . . . from even more embarrassment. I'd have died if I'd passed out in there." She tried to muster a smile. "I paid a fortune for this dress, and if I'd ruined it I'd have hated myself."

A sense of humor, too, Buck thought as they reentered the ballroom. From the instant he'd seen her, he'd been attracted to Amie. It was no wonder the TV camera had focused on her. She was not just beautiful; there was a quality about her that drew your attention. And the way she spoke her mind was a refreshing surprise. He was a bit disgruntled now that his plans to capture her were foiled. He'd honestly expected her to leave with him.

"Are you sure you feel all right now?" he asked.

"Positive. I'm not even dizzy any more," she fibbed.

Before she realized it, they were back at their table. Buck thanked both her and Tom for the dance, then turned his attention to Celia Stockton. When Amie glanced toward them, Buck's back was turned to her. She couldn't explain the hint of jealousy this aroused.

"So?" Tom asked with a raised brow.

"I admit the man's crazy," Amie said, "but he's a terrific dancer."

And all through the night, Amie dreamed she was dancing. Her partner's face kept changing, but the body was always the same. Rock-hard thighs pressed against hers, strong-muscled arms held her, and she could feel a heart beating against her breast in cadence with her own.

TWO

Amie drank her coffee and dressed hurriedly. She poked her head through the front door of her apartment to see what the weather was like. A cold, gray February rain drizzled on the concrete pavement outside. Mixed with it was sleet and an occasional snowflake.

From the closet she took her long, russet-colored wool coat, a heavy scarf that she wound around her head and let fall over her shoulders, and a big, brown umbrella.

The small reception room that served both Charlotte Crisis Housing and Charlotte Emergency Housing was overflowing when Amie got to work. The director, Marsha Dellinger, was waiting for her.

"It's impossible," Marsha exclaimed when Amie walked into her office. "We'll never be able to house all these people for the night."

"There's no such thing as impossible," Amie insisted.

"Tell that to the twenty or more out there in the waiting room," Marsha said. "We'll be lucky if we're able to put a roof over half their heads, and you know it. I've already called the Salvation Army, and the way things look right now, they may have to put everybody in the same room simply to keep them from freezing tonight. We aren't equipped to handle so many people, Amie, and the numbers keep growing."

By two o'clock the rain and sleet had changed to snow. With all her resources exhausted, Amie sat at her desk with her hands clutched in her lap. Emergency Housing, just a year old, could accommodate only four families and eight single women. "Our quota was filled a month ago," the agency's executive director told Amie.

It was no better at the Salvation Army headquarters. "There are so many more this year," she was told. "The way it looks, we'll have to pack the overflow into one room."

Dammit, what was she going to do? There was a pregnant woman in the waiting room, and Amie couldn't bear the thought of sending her to share one room with a host of other people. When the phone rang, Amie answered sharply, "Yes?"

"So, who took your candy? Buck Cameron?" came a teasing voice.

"Millie, am I glad it's you. I'd hate to have snapped at someone from city hall."

"Or at Buck?" Millie taunted.

"I see Tom's been carrying tales," Amie said.

"Ummm. Not exactly," Millie replied. "He did tell me he thinks Buck has eyes for you, and I thought maybe I should do my good deed for the day and steer you clear of him."

Amie frowned, wondering why Millie's remark rankled her. "What is it about Buck that makes you and Tom think I could fall prey to him? I've been around that block once, remember?"

"You know what they say, Amie. We tend to make the same mistake over and over again."

"Well, *they* don't know Amie Phillips. That's the kind of mistake I don't intend to repeat. You can rest your mind on that."

"But you did have a good time, didn't you?" Millie asked. "Tom said you looked smashing. Aren't you glad now that you have the new gown? What was Celia Stockton wearing?"

After filling Millie in on the details she could remember about the evening and promising to have lunch with her soon, Amie felt guilty for spending so much time on the phone socializing—rather than doing something productive about all the people who needed a place to sleep for the night. It had been a bit startling to realize that her most vivid memories of the past evening were of Buck Cameron. Everything else paled into nothingness.

Then a light flashed in her head. She remembered something Tom had said: "You never know, you could meet the very person who might help you the most the next time you need a big donation."

Amie put on her coat, wrapped her scarf around her head and then her neck, and clutched the handle of her umbrella. "I'll be back in a little while," she told Marsha.

On the eighteenth floor of the Cameron Building, Amie stopped in front of a huge, carved oak door. On a small brass plaque engraved letters read, J. B.

Cameron, Chief Executive Officer. Taking a deep breath, she turned the knob.

A young woman with honey-blond hair twisted into a bun at the nape of her neck peered through black-rimmed glasses at a shorthand pad lying on her desk. She looked up at Amie, not bothering to conceal her surprise. "Yes?"

"I need to see Mr. Cameron," Amie said, knowing she must look a sight. "Buck Cameron."

"Do you have an appointment, Ms.—?"

"Phillips. Amie Phillips. No, but I'm the assistant director of Charlotte Crisis Housing, and . . ."

"I'm sorry, Ms. Phillips," the woman said. "Mr. Cameron is very busy this afternoon. It will be impossible . . ."

"I *must* see him!"

The young woman only sighed and removed her glasses. "Who allowed you on this floor, Ms. Phillips?" she wanted to know. "No one is given a pass to the executive suite without an appointment."

While the woman spoke, Amie was looking around the large, lavishly appointed reception area. To her left was a wide expanse of windows with hallways that led to the right and to the left. "Yes, well, thank you," Amie said. "I'll call for an appointment."

Amie knew she was doing the right thing when fate stepped in and came to her aid. At that very moment the phone rang on the blond woman's desk.

With the receptionist's attention diverted, Amie eased quietly around the huge schefflera near the door and quickly decided to take the hallway to the left. Once she was in the clear she saw that there was yet another decision to make. Assuming she'd lucked out and taken the right hallway, which of the three doors would be the one to Buck's office?

Most likely the one at the end of the hall, since there was an exit sign nearby. Buck Cameron would undoubtedly want to be sure he could make a fast getaway if the whim struck his fancy. She opened the door and walked inside.

She didn't know what she had expected, if anything, but it wasn't this. The room was large, but not the least bit inviting. It was so formal and businesslike it . . . well, it didn't look like an office she imagined Buck would occupy. Anyway, it was empty. "I guess I picked the wrong door," she mumbled to herself.

"That depends on where you expected it to lead."

Startled, she looked in the direction from which the voice had come. Beside the panel of three windows in the room, almost hidden behind heavy, dark green draperies, Buck stood watching the snow fall.

He looked like anything but a CEO, dressed in dark brown leather pants, short boots, and a dark heather, turtleneck woolen sweater. He turned to look at her with the same blank expression he'd worn when he'd taken her back to her seat last night. She remembered how surprised she'd been; remembered her twinge of jealousy. Coupled with disappointment?

"What in hell are you doing in here?" he asked bluntly.

For the life of her, Amie couldn't say a word. He had to be the weirdest man she'd ever met. Eccentric? He wasn't eccentric, she thought, feeling her anger rise. At the moment he was being rude and, from the way he was glaring at her, he thought nothing of showing his anger.

She tried to concentrate on these negative thoughts, hoping they would have some influence on the unbidden response of her body. It didn't work. Not even the scowl on his face diminished its effect. It was a good thing the man couldn't bottle his sexual magnetism.

She kept telling herself it was only chemistry and that she had nothing to fear. Taking a deep breath, she reminded herself why she was there, making a concerted effort to get her body coordinated with her mind.

All those people waiting in the reception room at Crisis House were the ones who'd be on the losing end of the stick if she let him intimidate her or, worse, if she let herself be goaded into showing her anger. "I'm glad you've been looking outside," Amie said matter-of-factly. "You saw how bad the weather is, so you can imagine how cold it must be."

He stared at her as if he were seeing her for the first time. Amie felt herself quake. He didn't remember her!

Now what was she going to do? Despite the blow to her psyche, she decided to go ahead and ask for his company's help.

"What does the weather have to do with anything?" he asked. His eyes scanned her from head to toe, making her miserably aware of her less-than-glamorous appearance.

When he didn't move, she walked toward him, holding out her hand. "I'm . . ."

"For God's sake, Amie. It's been less than twenty-four hours since I held you in my arms. Surely, you don't think you need to introduce yourself."

Though he sounded impatient, he took her gloved hand. When he smiled, Amie thought it was the warmest smile she'd ever seen.

"Swaddling clothes and all," he said, charging her with his electric blue eyes.

She felt her cheeks flush, knowing how she must look with her scarf still wrapped around her head and her nose so cold it threatened to drip if it thawed—and that was a distinct possibility. Even through her woolen gloves, the heat that emanated from his grasp was hot enough to melt icicles. If that didn't do it, the look he was giving her was sending her old mercury right up to the boiling point.

Damn him. He didn't play fair. He thought he could ignore her one minute and turn on the charm the next. She withdrew her hand and fumbled in her purse for a tissue.

"How did you get past the receptionist?" he asked, still smiling.

"It wasn't easy." She wiped her nose and looked up at him. "I apologize for slipping in like this, but I'm desperate for your help."

His grin vanished and he motioned her to one of the uncomfortable-looking leather sofas. When she sat down, it felt as hard as it appeared to be. "I work for city government," she began. He nodded and Amie was even more aware of his discerning blue eyes. "Actually, I'm . . ."

"Assistant director for Charlotte Crisis Housing," he supplied. "My memory's not impaired, Amie." *Not in the least. I remember how perfectly you fit in my arms when I hold you. Exactly how our bodies move in perfect rhythm when we dance. I remember the excitement you stirred in me last night, just as you do this very minute.*

"I didn't tell you where I work, only that it was for the city."

"You didn't? Well, obviously you didn't come here on a social visit. So what, then?"

"You don't waste time getting down to business, do you?" she asked.

"Is it business we're getting down to? You disappoint me. But then, that's my own fault, not yours."

"I told you that I'm desperate, Mr. Cameron. If I weren't, I wouldn't be here."

"Buck," he said. "My father's Mr. Cameron."

"The receptionist said you were very busy." She wished she hadn't emphasized the word busy. If, for Buck Cameron, it meant staring idly through the windows, it was no concern of hers.

"The receptionist was right. She keeps her job by being right. I have some thinking to do."

"Then I'll get to the point. As you can see, we're having a winter storm. We have more people at the crisis center than we're able to accommodate. They're in desperate need of a place to stay, and I thought . . ."

"I'm afraid I can't help you, Amie. I'm not in housing. I'm in the department store business."

"If you'd let me finish!" she snapped. He couldn't dismiss her so easily. He had to help. "You've interrupted me three times already."

"I don't have time to listen to a sob story. I have some important decisions to make today."

"Damn it! You also have a warm home to go to when you leave here! Are you telling me you won't lift a finger to help? Even when you can take it as a tax write-off?"

With one sensitive finger, he traced the contour of her cheek. His unexpected touch was as electrifying as putting her finger into a light socket would have been. *Why?* she wondered angrily, when she was fast learning that he was everything she disliked in a person. She wanted to kick him when she heard his soft chuckle.

"Would you like to go with me? To my warm home, I mean? I can do my thinking there as well as here . . . probably better, with you there to give me inspiration."

"You're insufferable," she muttered, rising to leave. What did she expect from a man who could kill innocent wild animals for no more than the sport of it?

"Wait," he said, reaching for her hand. "Listen to me, Amie. Do you have any idea how often Cameron, Inc. is called on to make donations to more causes than you can imagine exist? We already give more than we're allowed to write off. And damn it, there are channels you go through. You don't come rushing into somebody's private office asking for a place to put people up for the night." She only glared at him. "And stop looking at me with those accusing green eyes as if I'm an ogre or something worse."

"I'm sorry I bothered you, *Mr. Cameron,*" she said curtly, jerking her hand free. Turning, she headed for the door.

"Listen to me, Amie," Buck said again, following behind her. "You can't afford to take your work this seriously. It's no wonder you were about to pass out last night. And here you are traipsing around in the snow when you could very well be catching the flu. Damn it, you'll have ulcers by the time you're thirty."

"They'll be *my* ulcers," she said shortly.

"And for what?" he asked angrily. "Don't you know the same people you find a bed for tonight will be looking for one tomorrow night and the night after that? If you don't learn to take it in your stride without getting yourself all worked up, you'll be living in a constant state of crisis."

How many times had she heard that? He was exactly like every member of her family. But as her brothers would say, how could she blame a man for voicing something he truly believed? "Damned right wingers," she muttered, grasping the doorknob.

Buck covered her hand with his. "Have dinner with me, and I'll tell you all about people and how they'll sap your life's blood if you let them."

Did he know he was sapping hers right now? she wondered, wishing he'd move his hand. She couldn't think clearly with him touching her. It numbed her brain. She supposed chemistry was a purely physical thing, having nothing to do with rational thought. Which, she warned herself, made it all the more dangerous.

"You know, Amie," Buck said with a slightly bemused expression on his face, "I find you very attractive, though I honestly don't know why. It's obvious that you have scruples, and women with scruples are dangerous. Not only are they adept at dropping snares over your head, they immediately set about trying to domesticate their captives. But I'll tell you what. Have dinner with me, and I'll even do the cooking myself. I'm willing to take a chance if you are."

"It may surprise you to know that I *don't* find *you* attractive," Amie blurted. "Furthermore, I already have plans for dinner."

"You're not a very good liar," he said with an infuriating grin. "You'll have to work on that. It's a skill you'll need to survive in your line of work."

"Is that so?" she asked sarcastically. "I doubt

that even a good lie would work on you, Buck Cameron."

Again, she attempted to open the door, but he only tightened his grip on her hand. Then, abruptly, he let go. "Oh, hell," he muttered. Turning, he walked toward the desk at the far end of the big room.

Amie quietly opened the door and walked through it.

"Where is she?" Buck asked, frowning as he scanned the reception room. How did she disappear so quickly?

"Where's who?" asked the receptionist.

He hurried past her to the door that led into the hallway and opened it, expecting to see Amie waiting for an elevator. There was no sign of her. Of the three elevators in use, one was on its way up, two were going down, and one of those was already to the third floor. He looked down at the check he'd written. "Stubborn damn woman!" he muttered.

But then his face lit with a triumphant smile. Life couldn't be easy for a do-gooder, and especially one as softly feminine as Amie Phillips. It would break her in no time, unless someone was around to hold the pieces together . . . and he couldn't think of a better person to do that than himself. At least for a while, his mind added instinctively.

"Mr. Cameron!"

Buck turned his smile to his secretary who was coming off one of the elevators. "Get caught in the storm?"

"Mr. Farber didn't have his proposal ready," she explained. "I knew you were anxious to decide on the changes for that pension plan this afternoon, so I waited."

"I've already decided," Buck said, walking beside Kristen Wells, the secretary who had been with his father before he retired. "I'm not going with Farber's plan. It may be good for the Camerons, but it isn't good for the employees. I like Ashford's idea—a combination of insurance and mutual funds. If we go with that, when an employee retires there'll be cash plus investments that will provide immediate income, or that can be left to grow in value for the later years. People retire too damn early now, and most don't realize they'll be around a good while longer."

Kristen patted Buck on the shoulder. "I knew I was wasting my time going to Farber's this afternoon. You get more like your father everyday, do you know that?"

Buck laughed. "Older, you mean?" He stopped and met Kristen's eyes. "Kristen, do you think I could get along with a do-gooder?"

"A what?"

"A do-gooder! Damn it, you know what that is."

"I guess it depends on who the do-gooder is."

"Do you ever give a direct answer?"

"Not to you or your father," she answered with a chuckle and another pat on Buck's arm. "Do you think I'm crazy?"

"It's still snowing," Buck observed when they entered his suite of offices.

"And it's coming down hard," Kristen said. "I really feel sorry for all the poor people who don't have a warm place to go home to."

Kristen made no comment when she took the mail from Buck's outbox at the end of the day and noticed an envelope addressed to Charlotte Crisis Housing.

Nor was she surprised. Like his father, Buck Cameron was an enigma to some, but to Kristen he was simply a complex man. She smiled, wondering about the *do-gooder*. From the way he'd looked when he spoke of her . . . and Kristen was certain it was a *she* . . . maybe he'd finally run into a woman who could simplify his life.

Shaking her head, Kristen looked back toward the storm that raged outside. It would take a special sort of woman, she thought. It would take someone way out of the ordinary to understand Buck Cameron, let alone love him. Without a lot of love and understanding, he'd be a hard man to take.

THREE

Buck rolled the slender gold pencil back and forth between his fingers and thumb. Idly, he got up and walked toward the windows. Evening was fast claiming the city. And a certain woman was claiming his thoughts.

Amie. Amie Phillips. Why couldn't he stop thinking about her?

Maybe it was because he didn't want to stop . . . because he was intrigued by the fact that whatever she stirred in him was more than his attraction to a beautiful woman, or even the excitement of pursuit. And Amie might not like admitting it, but she was as strongly drawn to him as he was to her. The evidence was all there—the way she sucked in her breath, trembling when he touched her, the look in her eyes when their gazes held, and the way her lips parted, invited, even when he knew she was angry with him.

Yes, their attraction was mutual. Of that, he had

no doubt. She was fighting it because of all the things she'd heard about him. If Tom and Millie Delahunt were her closest friends, Tom undoubtedly wasted no time warning Amie of his reputation. And there was Marsha. Of all the places there were to work, why did Amie have to be in the same office with Marsha Dellinger? Blaming him for her husband's death, she took perverse pleasure in seeing him suffer. Marsha would be the first to warn Amie against him.

Well, he'd be damned if he would defend himself. He was who and what he was, and that was that, take him or leave him. Most women didn't have a problem with that. But he suspected Amie was different from most women, which was why he wanted her . . . intended to have her.

He smiled, remembering how she'd looked bundled in that oversized coat with her head and much of her face hidden beneath the folds of her scarf. Right now, he had an obsessive need to unbundle her.

The snow fell hard and thick outside the windows. People hurried along the street below, some with packages in their arms, some with their hands deep in their pockets, and some walking along together, their heads close; no doubt anxious to get home where they would spend a cozy evening together in front of a roaring fire, make love, then fall asleep in each other's arms. A chill shivered down Buck's spine.

Millie was right, Amie told herself, turning onto her left side. She should think about getting out to meet some eligible men. At the rate she was going, she would be too old to have children by the time she got married. Of course, women were having first babies at forty now. Maybe they would raise the age limit again by the time she reached fifty.

After tossing and turning, she finally fell asleep; but sleep was as fitful as her wakefulness. Disturbing sensations tormented her restless body. In her dreams, the hard, naked body of a man stretched the length of her. The hot-blue eyes that looked down into hers belonged to Buck Cameron. His arms tightened around her and the deep stirrings he aroused were so real they woke her. Running her fingers through her thick, tousled hair, she wasn't surprised to feel that her scalp was damp.

When she bolted upright in bed, Charlie and Brigette, the two cats who owned her, stretched and looked at her curiously. "Sorry," she said, watching them yawn and curl back together on her bed.

Apparently, they weren't having the same problem that tormented her. There were times when being neutered didn't seem a bad idea.

After a glass of apple juice and a peek through the windows at the darkness that still hovered over the white landscape, she tried to sleep again. But Buck's insinuating laughter, the brooding look she'd seen on his face as he stood watching the snow fall outside his windows, the sparks she'd felt when his finger traced the contour of her cheek—they all combined to form a knot of frustration that twisted inside her.

When the phone jangled her awake, she realized she'd finally fallen asleep, despite her nighttime anguish. Charlie and Brigette leapt to the floor and dashed from the bedroom as if the phone's ringing were the last straw.

"That was quick," her mother said when Amie answered.

"Don't you ever sleep, Mother?"

"When you get old, Amie, you never know if you'll open your eyes again once you close them. I wanted to tell you to be careful getting to work in all that ice and snow. There were pictures of it on the early news, and the traffic on Independence Boulevard is awful. You aren't planning to drive, are you?"

"I'll catch a ride with the guy next door. I'm no more anxious to have someone slide into my car than you are to have me squashed."

"I called you yesterday when it began to snow," Lizbeth said, "but you didn't answer. Are you getting enough rest, Amie?"

"Mother, you know I take care of myself."

"I don't know," Lizbeth said, her voice tinged with concern. "Sounds as if something's ailing you."

Her mother could always tell when things weren't just right with her, Amie thought. She wondered what Lizbeth would say if she told her she had a big case of Buck fever. Most likely, she'd think her daughter had been deer hunting with one of her brothers.

"Yep, I guess that's what I have," Amie told Charlie and Brigette when she gave them their breakfast. "Buck fever."

"Look at that sunshine!" Marsha exclaimed as she opened the afternoon mail. "Maybe by tomorrow all this snow will be melted."

"Ummmm." Amie only nodded, trying to concentrate on the paperwork piled on her desk. She felt good about the way some things were working out. A family who occupied one of the four houses operated by Emergency Housing had moved into permanent quarters and the pregnant woman and her husband were being allowed to take their place. That was a relief.

"Ohhh, my God!" Marsha shouted, waving what appeared to be a check as she bounded from her desk. "Miracles never cease. Would you take a look at *this!*"

Amie's mouth dropped open when she saw the signature on a personal check drawn on the First Union National Bank. The big, scrawled letters were almost illegible, but she had no trouble making out *J. B. Cameron.*

"If you haven't seen a check with that many zeroes lately, it's for ten thousand dollars," Marsha sang rapturously. "*Ten thousand dollars!* Do you realize what we can do with this?"

So he'd come through, after all. Amie turned the check over in her hands, looking for the strings she knew must be attached. "There's something about Buck Cameron that really gets to me," she said, looking again at the heavy signature.

"Yeah, I know," Marsha said drily. "Some say it's his baby-blue eyes."

"*Baby* blue?" Amie couldn't help laughing. "I'll wager the only thing his mother has to remind her that he was once a baby is the hospital photograph they took when he was born. The minute that man opened his eyes, he must have put his baby ways behind him."

Marsha looked at her curiously. "You know Buck, then?"

"Not really," Amie replied. "I met him at the Heart Ball." She saw no reason to tell Marsha she'd gone to Buck's office to ask for a donation. If Marsha knew that, she could easily get the wrong idea, considering the size of his check.

Amie supposed Marsha knew the Camerons well, being a native of Charlotte. With one exception, she'd wager. From what she'd experienced so far, Amie doubted anyone *really* knew Buck.

"Are you alone?" Buck asked when Amie answered the phone two weeks later.

"Not exactly," she replied, feeling her pulse flutter. She had come to terms with the check he'd sent, deciding it was actually an impressive gesture, especially when he didn't believe in the causes he supported. Reluctantly, she accepted his right to his own beliefs even though she didn't agree with him. At least he'd given, and given generously. That was more than she could say for many of the big corporations who made their one-time donation to United Appeal and considered themselves philanthropists.

"What does that mean?" Buck wanted to know. "You're either alone or you're not."

"I suppose it depends on your definition of *alone*. Cats are very independent and mine like their privacy, so when they don't choose to be companionable, I consider myself alone. Right now, though, it's their dinnertime."

"Then you don't mind if I come over? I thought we might go someplace for a hamburger, if you haven't eaten yet."

A hamburger? The man made a ten-thousand-dollar donation to charity and then offered to take her out for a hamburger?

"That sounds good to me," she said. "It'll give me an opportunity to thank you for the donation you made to Crisis House."

"Ordinarily, I'd hold you to that," Buck said. "In this case, though, I'd rather you didn't thank me. Not for the check, anyway." Quickly changing the subject, he asked, "Are you sure a hamburger's all right? I don't have a lot of time or I'd suggest something else."

"I know a place in a shopping center nearby where they make terrific chili," Amie offered.

"You like chili on your hamburgers?"

"And onions, mustard, ketchup, and lettuce."

"I knew you were a woman after my own heart," he said with a chuckle. "I'm on my way!"

Amie wondered if she would have agreed to see Buck if he hadn't taken her by surprise. She wanted to see him, despite all the reasons she knew she shouldn't. How could they be friends when the only thing she knew they had in common was a taste for hamburgers? The fact that she craved his body was something else.

Zipping her jeans, she pulled on a long peach-colored sweater and hurried to answer the door. She had no idea what to expect since she'd seen Buck only twice, and each time the circumstances had been unusual. The only constant was the sexuality the man exuded. And that, she noted as she gazed up at him, was an understatement.

Buck stood in the open doorway grinning down at her as the wind whipped past him and into the living room. The light from the porch illuminated the brilliance of his eyes and spun threads of gold through his light brown hair. He was wearing a leather jacket with what appeared to be a hand-knitted cashmere scarf wrapped loosely about his neck. The scarf had a pattern of dark blue and burgundy diamonds, and the contrasting colors made his eyes bluer than blue. They were eyes with an impact that startled her.

"Hi," she said with hesitation, unaware that her voice was so low and breathy.

"Hi, yourself," said Buck, touching a cold finger to her cheek, offering a suggestive smile as he did so. "The car's warm, but you'd better get a coat."

"Well, yes . . . of course, I'll . . . I'll get a coat," she said, stumbling through the words. His touch, the way he was looking at her, the way his smile warmed her through and through—the last thing on her mind was a coat.

Once inside, Charlie and Brigette began their inspection of him. Charlie, perched on the arm of a chair, eyed him from head to toe; and Brigette made several small circles around his feet, then sniffed them. "Do they always do this?" Buck asked when Amie closed the door to the closet.

"Of course," she replied. "If you don't pass muster, they'll let me know."

"You trust their instincts?"

"Implicitly."

He took her coat and held it while she slipped her arms into its sleeves. Then slowly, he turned her toward him. The heat of his eyes made her heart skip a beat. She wanted to look away, but she couldn't. For an instant, she felt as if he had her under the sight of one of the powerful rifles she imagined he used to bring down his game.

"Don't," she said softly. "Don't look at me like that."

"Like what?"

"As if you plan to shoot me and then mount me in your game room."

"Ummm," he murmured, cupping her face with his hands. "Not yet, anyway," he said with a grin.

"You mean you'd consider it at some later date?"

His laughter was absolutely wicked. "Amie, I refuse to pursue a subject that can do nothing but get me into trouble. I adore word games, and the words you've given me have such endless and fascinating possibilities. I think our best bet is for you to lead me to those hamburgers."

He held her hand as they walked to the car, and when he opened the door he could smell the hint of perfume in her hair as he tucked her inside. She glanced upward, their eyes met, and she smiled. He felt a powerful urge to kiss her. He gave her hand a gentle squeeze, closed the door, and walked slowly around to the driver's side, hoping the cold night air would have a beneficial effect on his condition. This was one game he planned to win, and he meant to take it slow and easy, making no mistakes.

"Do you know where Eastway Shopping Center is?" Amie asked when Buck nosed his dark blue Mercedes onto Eastway Drive.

"I think I passed it on the way over here. Isn't it on the right as you cross Central Avenue?"

"That's the place," Amie said, staring straight ahead through the windshield. She hadn't quite recovered from the soaring emotion she'd felt when she had thought for sure he was going to kiss her. Or maybe the tingly feeling that played havoc with her senses was only from the deflation that came when he didn't kiss her.

"There's a hamburger place there?"

"A drugstore," she said, tilting her head to smell the strongly masculine scent that permeated the inside of the car. It was woodsy, yet subtly feral. "I discovered their hamburgers and hotdogs this past summer when I first moved here. Either they're the best I've ever eaten, or I'm always starving when I stop there."

The snack bar was at the rear of the drugstore. Buck guided Amie through the maze of aisles with his hand at the small of her back. A little pressure here, a little pressure there, and Amie knew exactly the direction he meant her to take. She remembered it was the same when they danced together. Following him was as natural as breathing.

"How do you know which way to go?" she asked, glancing over her shoulder to smile at him.

He wondered if she were a born flirt, or if she intentionally meant to vamp him with that intriguing smile of hers. "The onions," he said, angling his head to sniff. "They make my mouth water."

And you do a lot more than that to mine. "Wait 'til you taste them," Amie invited. "They're even better than they smell."

So much for slow and easy. "Then move along, woman! I can't wait much longer."

They chose one of the three booths against the wall.

"Hi, Amie!" the short-order cook called from behind the counter. "What'll it be? One of each?"

"Two of each," Buck called out. Looking at Amie, he grinned. "I see you're a regular here, so do you mind telling me what I just ordered?"

"Two hamburgers, two hotdogs, all the way. And we'll get big colas to wash them down."

"Think you can handle all that?" Buck asked, resting his elbows on the narrow table and taking Amie's hands into his.

"Like the man said, I have a healthy appetite."

She hoped he couldn't feel her hand tremble when his lips brushed her fingers.

"Cold?" he asked innocently. "Want me to slip your coat over your shoulders?"

"I'm fine," Amie said, knowing she'd betrayed herself. "Truly." But she wasn't fine and they both knew it. Her heart was pounding and she couldn't breathe very well. She stared into Buck's eyes and wondered why God hadn't made the sky that color.

"So, tell me about yourself," Buck said, grazing the backs of her hands with his thumb.

"There's nothing to tell. What you see is what you get."

"Promise?" His voice was almost a whisper, yet it was deep and challenging. His hands tightened and for an instant Amie thought the bones in her fingers would break. As he locked his gaze with hers, her eyes widened, watching his change to an electric blue. The muscles tensed at his perfectly chiseled jawline.

Though his mouth hinted at a smile, his eyes drilled into her. Unwittingly, she had dropped the gauntlet and there was nothing playful about his response. Ah, but this man knew exactly when to pull the trigger; and better, where to aim his shot.

The seconds ticked by as Amie absorbed the impact of the implosion. Parts of her anatomy melted while other parts either tingled or went rigid. The burn of his eyes made her want to dive into the deep end of an icy pool.

"Only if you don't hold me within a time frame," she said finally. Her eyes flashed with sudden amusement and, though she didn't mean it to be, her expression was both teasing and seductive.

"I hope I'm not so transparent all the time. A

woman likes to think there's some mystery about her.''

''So, what I see isn't necessarily what you are all the time, huh?'' He released her hands to twine their fingers together, held them up and slid his elbows across the tiny table, leaning forward to rest his chin on their hands. The gesture forced Amie to lean forward, too, and she could almost feel their lashes touch when their foreheads came together.

''Promises are too much like shackles, anyway,'' he said softly with a gleam in his eyes. His voice was half teasing, half serious. ''I'll take you any way you happen to be, Amie Phillips. Any way, anytime.''

Her lips parted slightly to accommodate her quickly indrawn breath. Their noses touched when she tilted her chin. ''Well,'' she said, drawing out her words, ''right now, what you have is one hungry woman and I do believe our hamburgers and hotdogs are ready.'' *And in the nick of time,* she thought as the waitress set a tray on their table.

''You said you moved here this past summer,'' Buck said when Amie began to divide the food on the tray.

She nodded, catching his eye. He was looking at her as if he were searching for something he hadn't yet found.

''Where did you live before that?''

''My mother lives in Pinehurst,'' she said, thankful it was a short sentence and allowed her to swallow afterwards. ''I lived there with her and my dad until I went away to school. After I graduated, I worked in Raleigh until the job here became available.''

''Then you moved here from Raleigh.''

"That's it," she said with a nod of her head. "My life's story. There isn't much to it so far."

"What you're really saying is that that's all you plan to tell me."

"Some things are best left unsaid," Amie replied, grinning when he wrinkled his nose. Her hotdog was half gone when she looked up and saw that Buck hadn't taken his first bite. He was watching her intently, his eyes concentrating on her mouth.

"What are you doing?" she asked. "Waiting to see if the food's poisoned?"

"I'm fascinated," he murmured, not taking his eyes from her mouth.

"You've never seen a hungry woman eat?"

"Not with such genuine pleasure."

"You won't be so fascinated when your hotdog gets cold," she said brightly. "I don't know why, but the hamburgers stay hot longer. I always eat my hotdog first." She took another big bite, eating it slowly, savoring the spicy mixture of condiments heaped on top.

Buck looked away from her mouth to see the sparkle of her eyes. "That's something else we have in common," he said.

His smile and his manner were both so relaxed, Amie had no problem accepting his observation. At the moment, she could easily believe they shared more than the great American pastime of gorging themselves with fast food. "Aren't you going to tell me what it is?" she asked.

"You're getting more pleasure from that hamburger than taste. You enjoy oral gratification."

"If you're going to analyze it," she said, grinning as she patted her stomach, "don't forget how good it is to have a full, satisfied belly. We got here in the nick of time. I was starving.'' She drank her cola and dabbed at her lips with her napkin. Resting her hands on the table, she leaned against the back of the booth. "Now it's my turn to watch."

He chuckled, and Amie knew again the potency of his smile. Despite the sexual chemistry at work, she was beginning to feel comfortable with Buck. He was showing her a side of himself she hadn't guessed at.

And maybe because of the chemistry and the fact that neither of them made a big deal of trying to hide it, she wasn't the least bit self-conscious about staring at his mouth. Well-defined and firm, his lips alone spoke volumes. They said he was stubborn, determined, yet sensitive, perhaps even vulnerable. Buck Cameron felt things deeply and was a very sensual man. She couldn't reconcile this with his being a big-game hunter. But, then, when she first saw him, hadn't she thought those lips could be cruel?

"Do you have any brothers or sisters, Amie?"

"Two brothers," she answered, looking up to meet his eyes. "One lives in Rockingham, near Pinehurst. Jason's a pediatrician. It's a good thing because he and Sarah, my sister-in-law, have four children and one on the way. He and Tom interned at the same hospital. That's how Tom met Millie, who has been my best friend since we were in high school. Adam and my other sister-in-law, Margaret, live in Atlanta and don't have any children yet."

She stopped, giving him a rather self-deprecating smile. "I could have answered your question with a simple yes. You didn't ask for my genealogy, did you?"

"I want to know everything there is to know about

you,'' he replied with genuine interest in his eyes. ''Even the part you avoided mentioning earlier.''

''Surely you don't mean to pry into my love life?'' She was laughing now, but she preferred to stay away from that subject.

''Love?'' he asked pointedly. ''Are you saying you've really been in love? The kind the poets embellish?''

Amie detected a measure of derision in his tone. It puzzled her. ''You don't believe in love?'' she asked.

Watch out for that snare, he warned himself. ''Do you?'' he countered.

''Of course I do,'' Amie replied. ''And the answer to your next obvious question is no, I haven't been in love. Not really.''

''And what does that mean, *not really?*''

Holding on to her wits, she tried to give him an honest answer. ''There was someone I was very close to, but . . . well, obviously we're not together any more. I guess I didn't like him enough to learn to love him. Or vice versa.''

He scrutinized her, wondering why he wanted to shake her. ''What the hell does that mean?'' he asked.

Growled, Amie thought was the best way to describe the tone he'd used to ask his question. He'd actually *growled* at her.

''Just what I said,'' she told him. ''To have a permanent relationship, I think it's just as important to like each other as it is to love each other.''

''And this someone to whom you were so . . . close?''

Amie laughed, knowing how absurd he must think

her reasoning was. "I guess it would make more sense simply to say no, I didn't love him."

The way Buck was looking at her struck her funny bone.

When she laughed again, he felt that same anger. At least he thought it must be anger, only he wondered if it were something else entirely. *Jealousy?*

He cringed. He'd never been jealous of a woman in his life. But why else did he want to shake Amie? From the way it sounded, this man had made love to her. And he didn't give a damn what they felt when they did it, he didn't like it. He didn't like it even though he knew he had no right to feel angry. Hadn't he done the same with many women, many times?

"How could you have thought you loved him in the first place, if you didn't?" he asked.

"How should I know? What difference does it make, anyway?"

"It upsets you," Buck said wonderingly. Was she still in love with the guy? Was this a simple case of denial?

"Of course it upsets me."

"Did he hurt you?"

"The only thing that hurt . . . still hurts . . . is the fact that I put so much effort into trying to make it work, when the truth was, he never expected it to work. Well, actually," she said, looking down at her hands, "I know now he didn't want it to work. Not permanently. All he wanted was an affair, and I didn't have sense enough to see that until it was too late."

"Do you still want him?"

Her eyes flashed. "No, I don't!"

"Then don't make it so complicated. Whether you

loved him or not isn't the point here. The crux of a relationship between a man and a woman is whether or not they want each other. It's that simple. Either you do, or you don't. Why do you have to complicate it with words like *love* and *permanence?*"

"You make it sound as if the sexual aspect of a relationship is all that matters."

Careful, his inner voice warned. "Show me a happy couple, Amie, and I'll show you a well-used bed."

She felt the heat rise to her cheeks, but she couldn't leave well enough alone. "And what about the rest?" she asked. "What about the head trip?"

"The head trip?"

"The liking, the mutual respect, the caring and compassion . . . all the things involved . . . the cerebral as well as the emotional."

This woman didn't mean to make it easy for him. "We're back to the liking bit, are we?"

"It can't be just sex. Not if it's going to last."

"Physical attraction can be a powerful thing," Buck suggested, drawing his thumb across the soft underside of her wrist. "Sometimes it's enough."

His touch made more than her wrist tingle. She looked up and their eyes met for a long, heated moment. *Worse than Joe,* Tom had said. Now she was beginning to understand the danger Buck Cameron posed. He had her believing him, when she knew he was wrong. Why couldn't he understand that desire alone was not enough to build a lasting relationship?

Then it hit her. "That isn't what you mean at all, is it?"

"What isn't?"

"You aren't thinking in terms of real love or a

permanent relationship. What you're talking about is lust, pure and simple."

Buck laughed, and its sound, Amie thought, should have been recorded. He could make a fortune selling it to the producers of videos, commercials, anything that sold blatant sex. But that was his specialty, wasn't it? That, and hunting wild animals.

She wondered why she hadn't seen the connection before now. She also wondered why just looking at him made the blood sizzle in her veins. Why didn't she make it easy for herself? She could play his game and simply seduce the man. Get him out of her system once and for all. The more she thought about it, the more it made sense. She would be the hunter, not the hunted.

FOUR

The hunter, not the hunted. Even its sound had a nice ring to it. "I won't say I disagree with you," Amie replied, shifting to C-gear. C, of course, for *crafty*. "Good healthy lust is far less complicated than trying for a serious relationship."

Ah, thought Buck. How clever of him to maneuver her into a more realistic arena of thought. They were finally at a common ground and, to be on the safe side, he'd do his best to leave it there.

"You mentioned your family," he said. "Do they approve of your work?"

Amie knew exactly what he was up to. She'd been pushing buttons that made him uncomfortable. He wanted to bury all that stuff about love and serious relationships and stay with the good healthy lust. Fine. It suited her fine.

"None of my family approves of anything that puts a deficit in the national budget, and finding people homes is costly," she replied.

"I take it you're a liberal?"

She didn't miss the gleam in his eyes. She'd bet her bottom dollar Buck's politics were conservative, despite his life-style. "I'm an Independent," she stated proudly.

Buck wasn't the least bit interested in Amie's politics. For the past hour he'd watched the fire flash in her eyes, seen gentleness soften her features, and been mesmerized by a mouth he knew was capable of dispensing ecstasy. He wanted to feel that fire, probe her softness, capture the ecstasy. He wanted to touch her, to taste her. Simply, he wanted her. "Are you ready to go?" he asked abruptly.

Their eyes met with intention, and the air became subtly electrified. Without a word, Amie slid across the leather-cushioned seat and Buck helped her into her coat. She waited while he paid their check and took a deep, jagged breath when his fingers locked with hers.

Once they were in the car, Buck reached again for her hand. "Now that we know each other better," he said in that soft, gentle tone she knew he must use to hypnotize women, "it would be nice if you sat a little closer. I'd like to touch you . . . feel you close to me, Amie."

Oh, Lord. Had she really meant it when she told herself to go full steam ahead? To get him out of her system? Or were they brave, silent words used to mollify the fact that Buck's only interest in her was physical? The traffic light at the intersection flashed red.

Buck's foot pressed down on the brakes and he drew her to his side. His breath was soft and warm against her cheek. She turned her face toward him and his lips brushed her mouth. The light changed, but his right arm stayed around her waist. Amie snuggled next to him, laid her head on his shoulder, and they drove in silence with only the whir of the motor and the hum of the tires to lull them.

The car stopped and she opened her eyes. "We're here." Her voice was soft, husky.

Buck cupped her chin in his palm. His face moved closer, so close she could see each long, burnished lash that framed his eyes. His right hand moved upward from her waist so that his fingers pressed beneath her breast.

The image of the red traffic light flashed before Amie's eyes. "It was fun having hamburgers with you, Buck," she said quietly. "I'll just slide out the door and run inside now. There's no sense in you getting cold when I can see myself to the door."

"There's no way I could get cold now, sweet Amie." He drew her even closer, stroking her cheek with one finger.

Buck Cameron was one smooth operator. Hamburgers. Hah! He was an expert at setting traps, and knew exactly the right bait to use. Amie imagined he seldom went hunting without bringing home a trophy. Well, this time, she thought smugly, he was in for a surprise. Part of her trap would be resisting his.

But, oh, she was tempted. She lowered her gaze from his eyes to his mouth. Her plan was perfect, but it had one flaw. Did she have the strength to resist him tonight?

Even if she capitulated, she couldn't let him bag her with one shot. She had no intention of becoming one of his trophies . . . mounted on a wall or a memento to be placed in a corner somewhere. Not again. She'd learned her lesson. Whatever happened between her and Buck had to be on her terms.

Swallowing hard, she summoned every ounce of will she possessed. Never, in her whole life, had she wanted to be kissed by a man so much as she wanted to be kissed by him. She knew, though, that one of his kisses would make her want much, much more. And the look in his eyes made it clear that he wouldn't make it easy for her to say no.

Buck's own thoughts were not standing still. His mouth descended and her mind went blank. She couldn't tell him to stop. His lips were taking hers and she lost all ability to verbalize. Her heart fluttered against her rib cage like a small, cornered animal incapable of discerning fright from the instinctive need for flight.

His voice filtered through her mind, calming, soothing. His breath caressed her lips. "Oh, Amie . . . Amie," he whispered. "I want you, Amie. Damn, I want you so much."

His fingers crept across her cheek, lightly stroking, then traced the fragile rim of her ear. Her breath caught somewhere in the depths of her throat as she moved her hand across his shoulder, upward, creeping beneath the soft wooliness of his scarf to touch the skin at the nape of his neck, to curl the hair that dipped just to his collar. Then her fingers curved around his neck, tentatively at first, then more surely, as if to anchor her floundering emotions.

His kiss began gently, almost tenderly. When she parted her lips, she heard the quick intake of his breath. The kiss deepened and he drew her hard against him, cradling her head with one arm. A sparkling cascade of sensation spread from her center outward, followed by a sharp, intense feeling of need.

Buck's arms changed positions, with one around her shoulders while the other held her just below her waist. His hand curled around to press against her belly and she moaned softly. No man had ever kissed her so thoroughly, and he knew exactly what to do with his hand to make her know how much more of him she needed.

When she gasped for air, Buck lifted his mouth to look at her. His expression was more arousing than the kiss. "I'll see you to the door," he said raggedly.

Amie nodded her head, and felt his hand tremble when he touched her cheek.

He took the key from her purse and unlocked the door. Carefully, he put the key back, closed the purse, and handed it to her. When their hands touched, their eyes met and Buck drew her into his arms again.

"Don't kiss me," she said weakly. It wouldn't be enough. One more touch and her plan would be foiled. She imagined he suspected she was fast losing all her will to resist him, and she couldn't let it be this easy. Her plan would collapse.

"Don't kiss you? I can't help it," he said in a strangled voice, drawing her bottom lip between his teeth. His tongue measured the opening between her lips, gliding from one corner of her mouth to the other. His arms tightened around her enough to hurt and his tongue thrust inside.

Her head fell back and she heard herself moan. It was a sound of surrender to the jolts of electricity that jarred her every nerve ending. She was oblivious to the danger of the sweetly langorous feeling now seeping through her. Despite the barriers of clothing, her body moved into his embrace, and when he took her hand and placed it between them she felt his hardness, the urgency of his desire for her. A cry of need pushed upward from the nether parts of her body.

Abruptly, she pushed away. Groping for the sanity that had escaped her, she swayed a little, felt his fingers dig through the wool of her coat as he grasped her shoulders. Peering up at him, she was disturbed by an uneasy, fleeting emotion she saw on his face before he quickly brought control to his features.

"No?" he asked with a tilt of his chin.

"No."

He bent and placed a quick, hard kiss on her swollen lips. "I'll call you, Amie."

She nodded slowly and watched him turn and stride quickly to his car.

Once she locked the door, she leaned helplessly backward against it. Easy, she thought with a degree of bewilderment. Too easy. One simple no and he was gone.

She raised a weak hand to her cheek. It was cold to the touch, but she was on fire. Every inch of her, she thought, and her mind as well.

Something soft and furry brushed against her ankles. Brigette gave a plaintive meow. Charlie only looked at her knowingly with his wide, golden eyes. Amie took a long, jagged breath and pushed herself from the door.

She'd have to do better than this. If she was going to be the hunter, she'd have to plan her strategy and work it to perfection, and she'd have to be careful not to become ensnared by her own plan. What she was feeling now was disappointment, and that wouldn't do at all. There was no getting around it.

She was up against a pro whose instincts just might be better than her own.

Almost three weeks later, Amie decided she'd been over-confident. Thinking how she'd planned to turn the tables on Buck, she felt foolish. Apparently, there were none to turn because she hadn't heard a word from him since he'd left her at her door.

One thing was for sure, it had been a searing encounter. But she kept remembering that unguarded moment when she'd seen something in his eyes she couldn't quite fathom. Was that the moment when he decided it was all a mistake—that he didn't want her enough to make an effort?

She knew he'd felt her melt for him. Was genuine emotion too tame for him? Or did he suddenly lose interest because he thought she was one of those women who said no while all the time she meant yes? Was it only the stalking that excited him? The capture? Had he decided that she'd be easy, simply because she'd responded in a way that she honestly couldn't help? Damn him, she'd said no and she'd meant it. Did he think she'd only been teasing?

"Oh!" She muttered aloud, clenching her fists. She wanted to hate him for reducing her to such thoughts. But despite her anger . . .

"Oh!" she muttered again, this time with a shudder, and this time the anger was directed at herself. She wanted him. She wanted Buck Cameron. She couldn't stop thinking about him and this caused her considerable agony.

To keep her mind occupied, Amie found herself on a roller coaster of activity. She often worked late into the night drafting a proposal for a plan that could more than double the available low-income housing in Charlotte. She visited her mother, and she actually accepted a dinner date only to find that it was Buck who occupied her thoughts all evening. She stopped by Millie's when she knew Tom would be late getting home.

"I don't mean to pry," Millie said to her on one such occasion, "but is anything wrong, Amie?"

"Why? What makes you ask that?" Recognizing the sharp tone she'd used, Amie apologized. "I'm sorry. I didn't mean to snap."

"I know you didn't," said Millie, watching her closely. "It's not your nature. That's part of what I mean, only it's more than your short temper. Something's really getting to you. If you'd like to talk about it, you know I'm all ears."

"Thanks, Beatrix Potter, but it's nothing, really."

Millie didn't push. Amie wished she could talk to her about Buck, but what could she tell her? That she'd danced with him once, been cradled in his arms when she'd almost passed out at the Heart Ball, had a rather jarring encounter with him over a donation she'd solicited, and that they'd spent a couple of hours together on an impromptu date? This, and she couldn't stop thinking about him? When it made no sense to Amie, how could she expect Millie to understand?

She didn't know how to explain her reaction to Buck's kisses, to the way she felt when he touched her with his hands and his eyes. She knew what Millie would say to that: "You've been too long without a man."

That, too, Amie thought with a wry grin. Yet she knew her lengthy abstinence had nothing to do with the way Buck made her feel. It was beyond explanation, beyond understanding when she knew, up front, that Buck was a man who enjoyed many women, never one.

A sharp, clicking sound caught her attention.

"I'm going out for lunch today," Marsha said, tapping her fingers on Amie's desk. "What time is your meeting with the Apartment Association?"

"Not until two," Amie replied.

"I'll be back long before then," Marsha said. "Why the long face? Worried they won't be receptive to your idea?"

"I'm trying not to think about it."

"Don't get your hopes up," Marsha cautioned, knowing very well that Amie's middle name should be Hope.

"I can't help it. And damn it, the plan's so simple. Half the members of the association own really big apartment complexes. When I surveyed them, I turned up twelve empties at Providence Square, so you can imagine how many there are all over town. While they're empty, I can't see why we can't use them, if it's only for one night. Imagine what it would have meant if we'd had fifty empty apartments during that snowstorm."

"I hope you can convince them."

"Just think. If they agree to let us use them, we could talk to religious and civic organizations and maybe get them to supplement the rent," Amie suggested. "Then some of our families could stay on a permanent basis."

"Now don't get ahead of yourself," Marsha warned, "especially when they're sure to think there's a catch in it somewhere." She looked at her watch. "Want me to bring you anything for lunch?"

"No, thanks. I brought mine so I'd have time to go over my notes one more time before the meeting."

Marsha laughed. "Amie, if you tallied up all the hours you've worked on that proposal, I'll bet you'd discover you're earning about twenty-five cents an hour at this job."

When Amie heard the door close behind Marsha, she checked her calendar to see what the rest of her week looked like. Not too bad, she decided, glancing out the window. There were only a few hours when her mind would be completely free to be plagued by thoughts of Buck.

She took out her proposal and looked at it. She knew Marsha was right. She was well aware that some of the members of the Apartment Association would skin a gnat to save a penny. They were always at odds with the Uptown Development Corporation, demanding to squeeze profits from any venture proposed even when, in the long run, the city could only benefit from the growth new housing development would bring. And that was why she was worried about her most important project, the one she hadn't told Marsha about yet.

She had her eye on an uptown site that, if properly developed, would go a long way toward solving the inner-city housing problem. She looked at the proposal she'd been working on that would utilize government subsidies as well as state and local involvement to build subsidized, low-income housing. It would take a lot of the homeless off the streets, and give others who were below the poverty level decent housing that was safe and clean.

But the big nut to crack in this instance would be the owner of the property. She meant to ask about the site at the meeting today. If the response was the least bit favorable, then she'd tell Marsha.

She looked out the window. The sky was the palest of blues and a canvas for the fragments of memory her mind painted with startling accuracy: the very first time she saw Buck at the Heart Ball; the way he'd looked at her that day in his office when she was certain he was going to kiss her, and the disappointment she'd felt when he didn't; the grinning caricature of a clown with mustard rimming his sensuous lips when they'd gone out for the hamburgers. And the way he'd kissed her when he took her home. Only fragments. Undoubtedly, the whole picture was something entirely different.

Who was she trying to fool? The article in yesterday's business section of *The Observer* made Buck's intentions where she was concerned unquestionably clear.

J. Wicket Cameron, Jr., Vice President of Cameron, Inc., announced this morning their board's unanimous approval of the corporation's extended pension plan.

Mr. Cameron gave credit for this innovative plan to his brother and the firm's CEO, J.B. "Buck" Cameron who, Wicket said, is the architect of the plan.

Revolutionary in concept, it is tied to individual trust funds that will guarantee all vested employees a degree of security from the time they retire until their death.

Buck Cameron, who is presently in Peru, was unavailable for comment.

He hadn't called to say good-bye. Amie supposed it never even occurred to him. Where was it written that a couple of hotdogs and one or two heated kisses cemented a relationship?

More than a thousand miles away, Buck was swearing beneath his breath. He walked to the open doors that led onto a small balcony from which he could see the proud mountains of Peru rise through the floating clouds. He laughed harshly. It was good to know something could still rise.

He thought about the woman Juan Sebastian had introduced to him. He remembered a time, a recent time, when she and other long-legged, beautiful women like her had offered all the excitement he'd needed from a companion. This woman was especially beautiful, so why hadn't he wanted her? What in hell was wrong with him? Had he lost his manhood?

He opened the closet door and began to remove his clothes. Throwing them across the bed, he bent to retrieve two bags he kept beneath it.

Buck knew the women he'd had in the past didn't love him any more than he loved them, but they had understood each other. They demanded nothing. They were always happy to see him and never complained when he left. They shared a certain attraction, had good, safe, and honest sex, and that was that. His life remained his own. No one infringed on his personal freedom and that was the way it had to be.

Not one of these women had ever threatened him with her crazy theorizing. He doubted a single one had ever given a thought as to whether she liked him or loved him. Simply, they wanted each other, and that's where it was. He didn't want a lifetime commitment. He wanted exactly what he was used to having. It lasted until the thrill was gone, and when it was over it was done. No regrets. No hard feelings.

Muttering a curse, he began to throw things into his bags. He put his camera equipment in its black leather case, then checked beneath the bed to make certain he hadn't left anything there.

Wasted! His whole trip had been wasted. Not even the big cats could hold his attention. In fact, he'd damn near killed himself trying to shoot that jaguar. He'd never before been careless when he went into the wild, and this time he'd broken the cardinal rule. He'd lost his concentration. He had to worry now that his mind had snapped.

It wasn't as if he didn't know what his problem was, and he knew what he had to do. Get Amie out of his system.

"So how did it go?" Marsha called from her office, perking up when she heard Amie come through the door.

"I'm not sure," Amie told her. "They set up a committee to study my plan, and they're supposed to let us know something by the end of next week."

She still didn't tell Marsha about her brainstorm. When she'd mentioned the possibility of developing the uptown property, the association hadn't completely thumbed it down. Some of the developers had actually shown a little interest. So, her next step was to go to the courthouse and get the property owner's name.

"Usually," Marsha said, "they put things off forever. To promise action within a week, they must have a serious interest in the plan."

Amie frowned. "I hope I didn't overdo my presentation. You know how I am. Sometimes I get started and don't know when to shut my mouth."

"Don't knock it," Marsha said with a wry smile. "It's something called youthful enthusiasm. I can remember being like that once upon a time before my fizz went flat."

Amie knew Marsha couldn't be more than thirty-five. She was a tall, lissome woman with closely cropped, naturally red hair. Her complexion was smooth and rosy as a peach. She had a good body, lean and firm. Amie wondered why she hadn't remarried since her husband died. "You can be very funny," she said.

"I can also be intuitive. I know you've been wrapped up in this proposal of yours, but something else is bothering you, dear Amie. Wanna talk about it?"

"No." Amie laughed when Marsha made a face. "It's something I have to work through myself. I'll get over it."

"*It* or *he?*" Marsha didn't look up as she opened the bottom drawer of her desk and put away the stack of papers she'd been working on.

"You know Charlie's the only man in my life," Amie replied.

"Yeah? What about Buck Cameron? I've been wondering about that check he sent. Maybe he succeeded in making an impression on you."

"Buck? Trying to impress *me?*" Amie hooted. "That would be the day."

"He's out of your league, Amie."

Amie's throat constricted at Marsha's words.

"Don't misunderstand me," Marsha added quickly. "You're worth fifty Buck Camerons. I'd hate to see you get hurt by somebody with his reputation, that's all."

Amie knew Marsha couldn't possibly know that she had ever seen Buck except on business. But she was right about one thing. Buck was out of her league. "I've heard he's a bit eccentric," she said, "but it's unfair to label him."

"He's labeled himself," Marsha replied. "His family name may put some people in awe, but Buck's never been part of the establishment, here or anywhere else. When it comes right down to it, neither has his brother, Wicket. Their father deserves all the credit in that family—he and their grandfather. They worked hard to build Cameron, Inc. and they both gave leadership to the state. But the sons? When have you ever heard or read about anything worthwhile they've done?"

"But isn't Wicket one of our senators?"

Marsha raised a brow. "I'll wager that you'd be hard pressed to find his name very often if you studied the congressional records. When Wicket goes to Washington, it's for little more than to enhance the family name. It gives them more clout here in Charlotte. But at least that's more than Buck can say for himself."

Amie studied Marsha curiously. "You're really down on him, aren't you? What about that donation you were so ecstatic about? Doesn't that count for anything?"

"People like Buck always have a motive. Ten thousand dollars is nothing to him."

"Come on, I can't believe that. And what if it is true? He made the gesture. The people it'll help don't care why he did it, and I don't see anybody else breaking down our door to offer their assistance. Give the man some credit!''

''Credit?'' Marsha put her hands on her desk and leaned across it. ''Let me tell you something, Amie. Buck Cameron's a first-class no-good. The only person he's interested in helping is himself. He could watch the homeless freeze to death and not lose a wink of sleep. That's why I know he had some other motive for sending that tainted check of his.''

Amie felt the blood drain from her face. ''I don't know why you hate him so,'' she said, stunned by Marsha's outburst, ''but you didn't seem to have any problem cashing that *tainted* check.''

''That money doesn't begin to pay his debts,'' Marsha said. ''But some day, he'll have to answer for the things he's done . . . the people he's hurt.''

Amie was on her feet, her face flushed and her hands clenched. ''If you're going to say things like that about him, the least you can do is explain yourself. You aren't being fair, Marsha.''

''I don't have to explain a damned thing,'' Marsha said. ''It's nothing against you, Amie. You don't know any better than to defend him.''

Amie felt numb when Marsha walked from the room. She knew that there was, or had been, something personal between Marsha and Buck. And whatever it was, Marsha hated him for it.

When Amie left work, she stopped off at the health club and put in her usual hour's time with the weights. It was a little after eight when she finally got home, and she was still thinking about the way Marsha attacked Buck.

She was also upset by her own need to defend him. Of all the men she'd ever known, Buck Cameron seemed the least likely to need defending. But she couldn't help wondering what had happened between him and Marsha.

When her doorbell rang, she glanced down at her faded yellow warm-up suit and the can of Fancy Feast she was emptying into Charlie's dish. After she'd taken her shower at the club, she hadn't bothered with her hair or makeup, and she knew she looked a sight.

The bell kept ringing. Brigette meowed as if to remind Amie that she came first. "Just a minute, baby," Amie said to the smaller cat. Setting the unopened can on a kitchen cabinet, she hurried to answer the door.

"I smell fish," Buck said when Amie opened the door.

Her heart lurched at the sight of him. How could he be more handsome than she remembered? His hair seemed a bit longer and it was mussed, as if he'd run his fingers through it. His blue cashmere sweater was a shade slightly darker than his eyes. And the way his jeans fit, she thought, should be against the law. How could a woman be held responsible for her actions, confronted by the likes of him?

She sniffed her hands. "Seafood Supreme," she said with a grin, wondering how many women met Buck Cameron at the door smelling like fish.

"You're just now feeding the cats?" he asked, taking her into his arms as he stepped inside. He leaned backward against the door to shut it, pulling her close to him. It never occurred to her to resist.

Buck looked down at her upturned face. It was flushed and her eyes were overly bright. Did it mean she was glad to see him? His soft laughter caressed her, just as his eyes and hands did.

"Don't you dare laugh at the way I smell," she said. "Let go of me so I can wash my hands."

"I'm not laughing at that," he said, tightening his hold fractionally, not about to let her go yet.

He wanted to feel her in his arms, to look at her face up close. He'd never seen her without makeup or with her hair damp, and she was even more beautiful than he remembered. She must have just taken a shower, or a bath, he imagined, thinking how tempting she must appear beneath a cloud of sparkly bubbles, especially a cloud of dissipating bubbles. He thought of her stepping from the tub. He could see her wet, naked body as he filled his arms with her, could smell her womanly scent, and feel her wet, slippery skin slide against his own when he filled her.

"As for my laughter, I was laughing because I'm happy," he said huskily, tracing the arch of her brows with the tip of one finger.

And he was happy, really happy, for the first time in almost three weeks. That revelation was enough to wipe the smile from his face.

"I've been calling you since a little after five," he said gruffly. "I decided I'd come on over and wait for you to get home."

"I've only been here a few minutes," she replied. It was on the tip of her tongue to ask why, if he were so anxious to see her now, he hadn't bothered to say good-bye when he left for Peru. And why did he think she was sure to come home? Or that if she did, she'd be alone? Did it never occur to him that while he was out stalking his women and wild animals, maybe she'd brought home a trophy of her own? Anger mingled with her desire.

"What if I hadn't been here?" she asked. "What if I hadn't come home at all?"

"I guess I'd have gone looking for you." As if her question had only now registered, he frowned and asked roughly, "Where would you have been all night, if not here?"

With her green eyes glittering, Amie thought of several short answers she might give him. But after weeks of silence, he didn't deserve an answer. Did he think he could drop in and out of her life on a whim?

"What are you doing here, Buck?" Stepping back from his embrace, she waited, her chin tilted proudly, her high cheekbones flushed. "Why did you want to see me?"

"That's what I came to find out."

Flickering light behind his blue eyes seemed to leap at her—flames or daggers, she didn't know which. Before possible answers could click into place, he grasped her arm, pulling her hard against him. Then both his arms were around her, crushing her slim body against his. When his mouth hovered over hers, she felt his male hardness press against her belly, making her acutely conscious of her body and the way he made it come alive.

"Buck . . ."

"Be quiet," he said in a gruff voice as his mouth closed over hers.

His kiss was hard, bruising, almost punishing. His tongue drove deeply inside her mouth, took possession of her, drained her of all thought and will. Her head fell backward and she surrendered to the onslaught of his hot, demanding mouth. His hands slipped beneath her shirt to caress the bare skin of her back.

"Amie . . . Amie . . ." His words were soft and then he was kissing her again. Now his lips were tender, his tongue searching, wringing every emotion from the corners of her mind, taunting, exciting her body. "Amie, God, Amie!" he murmured when she pushed half-heartedly against him. She needed to catch her breath.

But breath was replaced by something else, something as primal and, at that instant, as necessary for life. A tight, twisting knot grew deep and painfully inside her belly. It diffused a warmth that spread, grew hotter, twisted tighter, demanded more than mere air for breathing.

Amie's hands curled upward, twining themselves in his hair, and her body arched against him. He moaned softly while his hands moved over her breasts, then down the length of her body, then back to push inside the soft velour of her pants. Her hands tugged at his hair, then moved down his back to feel the tensile strength of muscles tensing and untensing against her palms. Buck's breath quickened in cadence with his treacherous fingers.

Amie's moan coincided with a screeching cry that came from the kitchen.

To shut away the interference, Buck turned her and leaned her against the door just as two flying balls of fur landed at their feet. Muttering a guttural curse, he pressed against Amie as if to shield her. His arousal was hard and pulsing against her thigh.

"What in the name of all that's holy . . . !"

When Amie managed to speak, the sound came as half sob, half laughter. "It's my fault," she said. Her face crumpled as she struggled with her unanswered need. "I should have opened her can of food before I came to the door." She pressed her ravaged lips with the back of her hand as if to still the trembling inside her.

"You mean she attacks you when she isn't fed?"

"She must have been trying to steal some of Charlie's," Amie said, "and he wasn't about to put up with that."

"And I'm not about to put up with this," he said with a heart-tugging smile. "Do you hear that, Charlie?"

"If he doesn't," Amie said, her eyes smoldering, "I'll explain it to him, loud and clear."

"Promise?"

Their eyes met and she took a long, choppy breath. "Promise," she said, as much to herself as to the fantastic, wonderfully seductive man looming over her.

FIVE

Buck followed Amie into the kitchen. She fed Brigette, gave Charlie a few extra tidbits to make up for what Brigette had gobbled up, and then she washed her hands. All this time Buck said nothing.

She dried her hands and turned toward him, catching her breath when their eyes met. His entire countenance had changed. There was no passion in his eyes, not a single trace of lust. But there was something else. And it frightened her.

Though she couldn't begin to know what lay behind his cool blue eyes, there was no mistaking the caution in Buck's voice when he asked, "Do you know why I came home? Why I'm here now?"

"I don't know why you came home," she said. "As for your being here, I thought . . . well, I thought maybe you wanted to see me. Why else?"

"Damn it, I don't know!" He took her by the shoulders, hard. His laser eyes seared through her. "I had an urgent need to see you, but I'm not certain why."

Amie burned beneath his scrutiny, but she didn't look away. He did want to see her or he wouldn't be here, would he? Why was it so hard for him to admit it?

Suddenly, it was as if a mask slipped from his face to expose his vulnerability. "Help me?" he whispered as his lips brushed a corner of her mouth. His lips moved slowly, soft as his warm breath to the other corner of her mouth. She tilted her head and his mouth angled to conform with hers, clung gently, then gradually opened. The tip of his tongue, firm and pointed, eased its passage between her lips and with an intensity that allowed no thought, only feeling, his mouth took hers.

Help *him?* Hot, bright flashes of light shot through her, and an exquisite desire that made her world spin crazily.

"Amie?" Her taste was on his lips, delicious, intoxicating. He knew this was what he'd been wanting all the time he was in Peru, only he wanted more . . . all of her. He *needed* more. He had to find out what made him want her so . . . why he'd never want another woman until he'd had Amie.

His breath still came in short, harsh pants. "Why, Amie? Why can't I get you out of my mind?"

Amie struggled to regain her composure. She pressed the back of her hand to her mouth. Her eyes flashed. A deep breath chopped through her. "I don't know," she said dazedly. "I guess for the same reason I'm having a similar problem with you."

Instantly, she wished she had bitten her tongue before making such an admission. But hadn't she decided she'd satisfy this crazy physical thing between them, then try to forget Buck Cameron? But it didn't seem right any more. What was wrong with her? Why couldn't she be consistent?

"I guess I'm not very good at this," she said, moving away from him when he relaxed his hold.

"At what?" he asked, eyeing her curiously. Even now, his desire hovered just below the surface of his forced composure, making the muscles twitch beneath his smooth, well-tanned skin.

"Forget it," she said. Pivoting, she turned from his gaze.

He followed her back to the sink where, as if in a trance, she soaped her hands again, then rinsed them beneath the faucet. Only then did she realize she was washing them for the second time. What would Freud think about that? she wondered, wishing she could make sense of the turmoil in her mind.

Leaning against the kitchen counter, Buck picked up a towel and took her hands, drying them slowly, finger by finger. Then she startled him by whirling away.

"I saw in the paper that you were in Peru," she said, turning to look him straight in the eyes.

Buck took another moment to gather his wits. What was this? Was she upset because he left without telling her? Well, of course! It clicked right into place, didn't it? Already she wanted strings on him.

He'd had his reason for leaving Charlotte so abruptly. He'd had a revelation that night on her porch when she'd surrendered so sweetly, so completely to his kiss. She'd said no to more, but even then he knew she was vulnerable. And he'd guessed something more. This woman was dangerous. He'd known then that if she ever decided to put her sight on him, he'd be a goner.

Then, in Peru, he'd had to face up to the knowledge that no matter how much distance he put between them, it wouldn't help. She'd already put her mark on him. So maybe that was why he had to come home. To find out just what kind of spell she'd woven and find a way to undo the damned thing. He wanted to be free again. Was that asking too much?

Still watching her intently, he said, "I needed to get away for a while. Sometimes, when I think I can't bear another day of civilization, I go there, or to Africa."

"To Peru or to Africa," Amie said slowly. "Well, why not? A little trip to the mountains or wherever does us all good once in a while."

He met the teasing laughter in her eyes and grinned back at her. "From what I hear," she said, "Peru's your favorite hunting ground."

"From what you hear?" He was right. Amie was being warned against him. So why didn't she run? That would solve his problem, wouldn't it?

But he couldn't forget how he'd felt a little while ago when she opened the door and he saw her standing there. It was as if everything inside him opened up to her. And when he held her in his arms, kissed her and felt her quick response, it was as if she'd filled all his empty places—and he wanted to fill hers. Literally *and* figuratively.

"Tom mentioned it the night of the Heart Ball," Amie continued. "He said you shoot wild animals there and in Africa."

So she wanted to change the subject. Fine. Fine and dandy. "Come on, let's go back inside," he said.

Amie followed him from the kitchen back into the living room and took her distance on the sofa. There was nothing defensive in his attitude. If anything, the tilt of his head and the expression in his eyes reminded her of the first time she'd seen him. There was a certain arrogance, or perhaps defiance, about him.

So, why don't you simply take him off to bed, get him out of your system, and then be done with him? she asked herself. "So, tell me," she said, "do you really prefer South America?"

"The two continents are very different," Buck said, feeling himself relax a little. "There's still a wildness about Peru that's slowly fading from Africa, but I'd be hard pressed to say one outranks the other as a place of beauty. It's the wild, free, natural state of existence that I can't resist . . . and the animals, of course. Especially the big cats. They make me feel humble, remind me of my mortality, give me a new zest for life."

An excitement began to creep into his voice that Amie hadn't heard before. That, and something more that shone in his eyes made her suddenly conscious of the great gulf she knew lay between Buck and herself. She could never share his intense feelings about the wilds of Africa and Peru . . . at least not for the same reasons. If she were there, she'd be looking for something far different from the kill Buck went after. Where was the thrill in that? she wondered.

She shuddered. His mind was not with her now, but on the plains of Africa or in the jungles of Peru . . . with a rifle in his hands.

An alien emotion chased through her. She wondered if what she felt was akin to fear, and if this was the thing about him that fascinated her. Could it be that Buck was to her what the big cats were to him?

"They're both exciting in their own ways," she heard him say. "I guess Africa's more compelling. There's nothing quite so thrilling as a thunderstorm as it begins to build up over the grasslands of the Mara." His voice was strangely vibrant, his eyes translucent when he explained: "Mara is in the southwestern part of Kenya, on the Tanzanian border. Masai Mara National Reserve covers 645 square miles, and it's one of the richest wildlife areas in Kenya."

He paused, aware of the tension that hovered about Amie. "What is it?" He leaned forward, taking her hands.

Amie didn't want to hear about the animals he'd killed. It frightened her to think such a man could make her feel the way Buck did when he kissed her; the way she felt now, watching him, listening to him. "It's nothing," she said evasively. "I don't mean to interrupt, but I was wondering if you've had dinner."

"I went straight home from the airport," he said, curious as to why she seemed uncomfortable with the present subject. It was her doing, after all. If they hadn't changed the subject in the kitchen, they might be in bed by now. Then he'd know for sure that she was just like any other woman in the throes of passion. They could sate themselves, put this crazy thing into perspective, and go on with their lives. He refused to believe it would be any different.

"Then you've had dinner?" Amie asked again.

"When you didn't answer your phone, I called my parents to let them know I was back, then kept trying to reach you. I snacked during all that time." He lifted her hand to his lips. Taking one of her fingers into his mouth, he bit gently. "I could do with dessert, though," he said, drawing another finger between his lips. "But what about you? If you haven't eaten, we could go someplace." Again he nibbled at her fingers.

Amie tried to deny the sharp thrill coursing through her. "Lunch was my main meal today," she said, "and I had a little something while the cats were eating their dry food. Charlie's on a diet, so I've been trying to take the edge off his appetite with the dry stuff before I give him his Fancy Feast."

Buck touched her cheek lightly with one hand. She was about to ask him why he kept looking at her as if he didn't know what to make of her.

He was about to ask her why she kept looking at him as if she were suddenly afraid of him.

Then he yawned, and Amie noticed the dark circles beneath his eyes. "You must be exhausted," she said, smoothing a lock of hair from his forehead. "You should be home in bed."

"I've missed you," he said, letting his eyes close. "Needed to see you."

"I missed you, too," she admitted as one of his arms reached for her, then drew her close.

When she leaned her head on his shoulder, the tip of his tongue traced the line of her jaw. She shivered, arching her neck, and felt his lips brush feather-light kisses along its slender curve. A tremor chased its way beneath the silken smoothness of her skin and his hands followed it, gently here, a light stroke over and beneath her breasts, a squeeze there, until his hand reached her firm, flat belly where it pressed, kneaded, making parts of her rise to the touch of his palms while other parts tensed, contracted, made her hurt for him.

When she thought she'd reached the limit of her endurance, she felt the stab of his tongue between her lips. She opened to him, inviting his hungry exploration of the texture and taste of her lips, her tongue, her mouth.

His kiss was hard, deep and taking. Then it was gentle, filling, all-giving. She heard the rasp of the zipper at the neck of her velour pullover, felt his hands on her bare skin. A soft moan caught in her throat as she thrust her breast into his open palm. From the sensitive peaks of her nipples, convulsive sensations spread through her body, and when his hand moved lower she gasped for breath beneath his sensuous mouth.

"Don't . . . please . . . don't," she murmured.

"You know it has to happen," Buck said softly, taking a long, deep breath. "We have to know."

"Know?"

"I don't need to tell you what I mean. You know as well as I do."

Buck was right. Was it not the same for her? Hadn't she already admitted to herself that this feeling between them couldn't be denied? Hadn't she decided to do whatever was necessary to get him out of her system?

But what if, for her, the emotion that churned inside her was more than just a sexual thing? If that were true, going to bed with Buck would be risking another relationship that could only hurt her. This time, with this man, she had no doubt that the hurt would be devastating. It was this thought that made her hesitate.

What is it? Buck wondered, taking her face gently

between his hands. Why was she suddenly so tense, so . . . Yes, she was frightened.

"Amie? Surely you're not afraid of me?"

"No, of course I'm not afraid of you." Not you, but myself. "It's . . . I don't know if I'm ready for this."

His lips brushed her mouth, light as a whisper. "Don't push me away, darlin'," he said in a choked voice. "I came thousands of miles to make love to you."

Drawing her closer, he sensed her effort to resist, but when he smiled and looked into her eyes he felt only a soft compliance. "Amie, try not to judge me when you know so little about me," he said quietly, aware that for the first time in his life he wanted a woman to do more than melt for him. He wanted Amie's understanding, her acceptance. And he didn't like it. It made him vulnerable, and that's the last thing he wanted.

Helplessly, she looked at him. With one hand, he drew her head back to his shoulder. Her arms crept around him, holding him while they sat for long moments, their soft breath the only sound.

Finally, Buck held her back a little and kissed her very lightly on the forehead. He felt her tremble. Amie was fearful of him, and he supposed it was no wonder, with all she must have heard about him. But he knew she wanted him despite her fears and her reservations. He also knew he'd never get her out of his system if she came to him with the least reluctance. When he made love to her, she had to want him as much as he wanted her, completely and without reservations. He meant to have all of her.

Smiling into her eyes he said softly, "I should go home so we can both get some sleep."

Amie said nothing, only closed her eyes when he stroked a wisp of hair from her cheek.

"I shouldn't have come over here like this, taking you by storm. I'd like you to come to my place for dinner tomorrow night. Will you do that?"

"Can you cook?" Her voice squeaked and they laughed.

He traced her smile with the tip of his finger. His voice was still husky when he told her, "I can do lots of things you don't know about yet."

Again Amie pressed her eyes shut. Like a wind chime, just the sound of his voice, his merest touch, and she tingled. "Do you really think we should?"

"Have dinner together?"

The look she gave him was wilting.

"I definitely think we should," said Buck.

"You're in a good mood this afternoon," Marsha said as she poked her head into Amie's office. "It's been a while since I've heard you singing to yourself."

Surprised, Amie smiled at Marsha. She'd meant to ask Buck about Marsha last night, but then, she thought with a smug little smile, she'd had better things on her mind.

"I have some good news," she said.

"You've met a new man?" Marsha asked brightly.

"Better than that. The chairman of the Apartment Association called. He wants to see me tomorrow morning."

And she couldn't wait to tell him that she was almost certain they'd be able to get the land they needed. Two hours searching titles at the courthouse had turned up only two names. A real estate developer owned a third of the property. Cameron, Inc.

owned the other two-thirds. And she was having dinner with Cameron's CEO tonight.

"I've been in a board meeting all afternoon and didn't have a chance to call you," Buck said when Amie answered her phone later that afternoon. "Are we still on for tonight?"

"Of course."

There was a smile in his voice when he spoke again, and Amie hoped she hadn't sounded too enthusiastic.

"I'm running late," he said. "Will seven-thirty be all right?"

"That's fine. It'll give me time for a long, hot soak in the tub."

His imagination did a flip-flop. "Unfair," he growled. "Don't get me all hot and bothered right now, sweet Amie. I have lots of work to do."

"Well, don't wear yourself out," she said with a chuckle. "I have some business to discuss with you tonight."

"Do that again."

"Do what?"

"Laugh. I love the way you laugh, darlin'. It makes me feel all warm inside and helps me forget that there are nuisances like board meetings."

Amie could almost see his lazy smile. The image made her forget everything except that they'd be together soon. Funny, she thought. When there was a reasonable distance between them, she seemed to forget all the reasons she shouldn't get involved with him.

"It isn't fair to flirt with me over the phone, Buck," she said softly.

"It's worse to tease, darlin'. I'll have to get even with you for that. See you soon."

"You live out here?" Amie asked when Buck turned onto a dirt road a good thirty miles outside the city.

"No, darlin'," he said, looking up through the tops of the tall pines that lined each side of the narrow road. "I'm taking you to the woods to ravish you."

Amie smiled and leaned her head against his shoulder. She looked out through the windshield and saw only woodland, a sky spangled with stars, and the full moon that led them down the bumpy dirt road. There was not a house in sight. "Don't you ever get lonely way out here?"

"Lonely? We're born of loneliness, Amie love. Don't you remember the soft, wet darkness of your mother's womb? By the time you fought your way out of there, loneliness had been conquered."

"I thought the womb was our last bastion of security, and now you're trying to tell me we were lonely there?"

"I don't know what in hell I'm trying to tell you," he said, laughing at himself. *Except that I want you, Amie Phillips.* "I do believe that if you're in tune with yourself, then you can't be lonely. Yet, I know there's something . . . Have you ever watched a magnet attract little slivers of metal?" he asked. "Sometimes I have the feeling there's a great big magnet somewhere out there that's pointed straight at me. It keeps pulling at me, but I never seem to be in the right spot for it to get me."

"So you keep searching for that spot?"

"Not really. I figure when the time's right, I'll step right into the middle of it."

"So, what are you, if not lonely?"

"Sometimes I feel driven."

Amie detected a note of sadness in his voice. She wished she could erase it. It didn't seem right for sadness to sit on the shoulders of a man as vital as Buck.

The night air was still cool, and in the dark interior of the car, Buck's closeness was a tangible thing. He squeezed her hand and laughed, as if he'd been reading her mind and refused to let anything dampen their spirits. This warmth pervaded her senses, filled her with an elixir that changed blood to fire, all emotion to desire, and made the unreal real—a lovely fantasy.

As if by magic, the forest opened and there were rolling hills dotted on each side of the road by lakes whose surfaces shimmered with moonlight. Amie stole a glance at Buck's profile and saw it as an outline against the star-bright sky.

"I'm driving in a race at Daytona next weekend," he said unexpectedly. "Want to come with me?"

"You're *what?*"

"The pit crew might even let you hang out with them. You can make sure they do it right, if I need to have a tire changed."

"I didn't know you raced," Amie said, swallowing the lump in her throat. Wild animals, and now this? How could a woman ever feel secure with this man? The closer she got to him, the more he frightened her. Why couldn't his passions be golf or tennis, maybe a weekend of backpacking?

"I don't follow any regular circuit," he said lightly. "I go in as an alternate sometimes."

"Thanks, but no thanks." After a moment's silence she said, "I suppose you hang glide and all that other stuff."

"Hang glide, yes, but I'm not sure what you mean by *all that other stuff.*"

"You don't really, do you? Hang glide, I mean." She wished he wouldn't joke about the dangerous life he led. More than that, she wished she knew what drove him.

"Yeah, I do, really," he said, glancing toward her. "What are your hidden passions, Amie?"

You. "I think I told you once," she said, smiling to herself. "There isn't much more to me than what you see."

"You're holding out on me, darlin'," he said with conviction. "Something puts the magic in your eyes. And sometimes you take a little gasp for air as if something just took your breath away."

"That must be indigestion." What did he expect? That she'd admit the effect he had on her?

"I'll just have to find out for myself."

The way he said it, she had no doubt he meant to do exactly that. "I'm afraid you're looking for something in me that isn't there," she said, turning to see a flash of moonlight touch the shadow of his smile.

"Your brand of excitement isn't for me, Buck. I like solid ground beneath my feet. Heights make me lose my breath and going too fast frightens me. I'm more at ease when I know what's on the other side of the hill, and then I like having a map in case I get nervous about where I'm going."

"All you need is an experienced guide," he said, releasing her hand to put his arm around her shoulders. "I don't believe you, anyway. I know the quest is as strong in you as it is in me, Amie. I feel it."

They fell silent. The car began to ascend a gently sloping hill. Amie stared out the windshield at the face of the moon, and they seemed to be heading straight toward the heart of it.

"We're each looking for something different, Buck," Amie said quietly.

"And what are you looking for, Amie? What, exactly, do you want?"

"I want to be happy."

"Ah, yes. Happiness."

"And you don't?"

"Don't want to be happy? Sure. I'll take happiness if you can tell me what it is."

"I'm happy now," she said in a soft whisper.

She heard the quick intake of Buck's breath, then its slow, steady release. When he spoke, his voice was deep and resonant, and filled with conviction and purpose. "I'll be happy when I make love to you."

Amie stopped breathing. She knew she was caught in the eye of a storm.

SIX

"Well, there it is—my sanctuary when I'm in Charlotte."

Like part of the landscape, rough-hewn wood, native stone, and areas of glass blended with the sloping hillside, merged with the encroaching woodland, opened itself to the moonlight and to the sparkle of the stars. It was definitely Buck's house.

"Better follow behind me," he suggested when he unlocked the wide front doors and pushed them open. It didn't take long to understand why. The minute they stepped inside something big, black, and shaggy appeared from nowhere, hurtling itself at Buck with so much power and excitement it almost knocked him down.

"Whoa, boy!" Buck tousled the fur on the big dog's head. "Down, now, and see who's here!"

Before Amie could take refuge, the dog was making its move toward her, but Buck stopped him with a clipped command. "Amie, this is Stranger," Buck said as the dog settled on his haunches. ''Tell Amie you're glad to meet her, boy.''

Taking the dog's outstretched paw, Amie looked curiously at Buck. ''Stranger?'' she asked.

''He showed up one night about six years ago. There was ice on the ground and his feet were in slivers, so I figured he must have been outside for quite a while. I took him in, cleaned up his paws, and fed him.

''He stayed around a few days and then left about a week before I was scheduled to go to Kenya. I asked Luke, the man who looks after the place when I'm not here, to look out for him, but he stayed away until I came back home. After that, he'd come around for a few days, then a few weeks at a time. Then one day he decided to stay.''

''Didn't you try to find his owners?''

''I asked around; even put an ad in the paper, but no one ever contacted me. I decided he'd been abandoned and had been foraging the countryside, hanging out with first one family and then another. He always seemed to be well fed. But I don't think he's ever belonged to anyone but himself. He must have sensed I understood that. I don't believe he'd have stayed, otherwise.''

''So I'm not the only one who takes in the homeless.''

Buck grinned and patted the dog on the head. ''This was different. Stranger adopted me, didn't you, boy?''

Amie followed Buck and his dog through an archway that led from the foyer to a large room beyond. The ceilings were very high and supported by great, rough-hewn beams. One entire wall was given to a huge fireplace made of the same native stone used for the wall. The floor was made of wide, softly polished oak planks, and several beautiful, hand-loomed wool rugs were scattered about.

The three walls that were not stone were constructed of the same warm, dark oak as the floors, and wide panels of textured, earth-tone silk show-cased striking photographs of wildlife—some of the most evocative work Amie had ever seen. "These are really wonderful," she exclaimed. "Who did them?"

"They're mine," Buck said with surprising modesty.

For a minute she was stunned. To do work of this quality he had to have a deep understanding of animal life. How, then, could he bring himself to shoot one?

"What are these?" she asked, pausing before a scene that showed thousands of strange-looking beasts attempting to cross a wide, rushing river. Many were still massed on the shore, some were thrashing about in the river, and one was in midair, plunging from the steep bank into the water below.

"Actually, they're gnu, or African antelopes, but they're commonly known as wildebeest. This was taken at the First Crossing on the Mara River. Every year, usually sometime in August, they head for one of the crossing points and begin their annual migration to the Serengeti plains in search of fresh water and food. I spent almost a week waiting to get this scene."

Buck stayed close beside her as she moved from one panel to another. "That's a young jackal," he explained when he saw her smile at the tiny head peering from the entrance hole of its den. "You see, its mother taught it well. It's checking the scent of the air to make sure it's safe to leave its den."

Amie could see only its eyes and its alert, pointed little ears.

"Here," Buck said, leading the way to the next panel where two small jackals frolicked on a bed of grass. "There were two in the family, a brother and a sister."

When she came to a magnificent pair of lions, Buck laughed and tousled her hair. Much the same as he had done to Stranger, she thought. And then, realizing what the lions were about, she hurried on to the next photograph.

"I don't think they'd mind you admiring them, Amie." Buck's voice was softly teasing. "He's one of the bravest, and certainly the most handsome lion in the Mara, and his mate's very proud to be making love with him. After dinner, I'll show you photographs of the cubs that resulted from their mating."

"They mate once a year?" she asked, trying not to appear as foolish as she felt.

He grinned at her embarrassment. "Once every time the notion strikes. On that particular day, when it was over, the female rolled over on her back and stretched all four legs in the air. When her mate lay down beside her and nuzzled her behind her ears, she rolled to her side, put her head between his two front paws, and went to sleep. He looked out over the edge of the cliff for a while and then decided he'd take a nap, too."

Buck chuckled and took Amie's hand. "They're not all that different from us, you know. Don't you enjoy a nap after having good sex?"

Seeing the bright spots on her high cheekbones, he gave her a hug. "Come on, I'll put dinner on the grill."

Amie glanced around once more before she was

willing to be led away. It was such a powerful room yet, at the same time, there was a peacefulness about it. But there was something . . . "Buck, are you re-doing this room?"

"Re-doing it?" He looked puzzled, then began to laugh. "Why didn't you come right out and ask? What you're wondering is . . ."

"Where's the furniture?"

"Except for some speakers in the wall that are connected to the stereo system, there isn't any," he replied, leading her down a wide hallway lined with more photographs. "You don't like it?"

"I don't know," she admitted. "I . . . well, I do like it. Only it takes some getting used to, I suppose, unless you meant it to be only a gallery for your photographs."

"I didn't mean for it to be anything except what it is—a room. That's all, just a room in my house."

"Oh," she murmured, still not quite understanding why he would have such a big empty room. A little one, maybe, but that room was at least thirty feet long.

"I like wide, open spaces," he said, as if that should be explanation enough for anyone.

The hallway opened into a kitchen-dining area of normal size. Buck took two veal steaks from the refrigerator and put them on the smokeless grill that was set in an island in the middle of the cooking area. "I hope you like veal," he said.

"I love it. What can I do to help?"

"You can take the salad from the refrigerator. All I promised was that you wouldn't go hungry, remember? I'm no gourmet cook, as you'll soon find out. When I make anything besides burgers, it means

I'm going the whole nine yards to make a good impression."

"I won't be impressed until I see your Christmas tree."

"My Christmas tree?"

"You're a legend around town, you know," Amie said, placing the big bowl of mixed greens and vegetables on the butcher-block table. "One of the first things I heard about the Camerons was that you keep your tree up the year 'round."

Buck turned the steaks and walked over to the table where Amie stood watching him. He wondered how much longer he'd be able to keep his hands off her. "That goes to show you," he said, dropping a kiss on the tip of her nose. "You can believe only half of what you hear."

His lips brushed her forehead, then her cheek when she tilted it upward. "Well, maybe two-thirds," he murmured, making her heart race when he nibbled at her earlobe.

"I left for Peru rather abruptly one year during the holidays and didn't get back until the end of January. That tree was about the brightest thing in my life then, so I decided I'd keep it around for a while. If I'd known it was the talk of the town, I'd have put it in the atrium and kept it decorated rather than plant it outside."

Buck's breath was warm and caressing against her neck, and when he began to nuzzle her playfully beneath her chin, she struggled to control the strong response she felt. She wanted to touch his mouth with her lips. She wanted him to take her into his arms and see where the waves of desire rushing through her would lead. "Something's burning," she said, shivering with a sensual delight. "You'd better check the steaks."

"Huh-uh, not the steaks," he murmured hoarsely, kissing her again briefly, this time on her mouth. Her body arched against him and she felt his fingers tighten, heard the quick intake of his breath, and saw the question in his blue eyes.

But he didn't wait for her reaction. As quickly as he had kissed her, he turned away and covered the short distance to the grill. With her heart fluttering in her throat, Amie touched a hand to her damp forehead.

"Will you hand me a plate, Amie?" he asked in a still rough voice.

"I hope you're not planning to put any rich sauce on the veal."

He grinned. "I'm a purist as well as a minimalist."

When she handed him the plate, their hands touched lightly. Amie was certain she could see the sparks fly. "What do you like on your salad?" Buck asked, letting his eyes warm her from her head to the tips of her toes.

"Vinegar and a little oil," she replied, taking a quick, short breath.

"How's safflower?"

"That's what I use at home."

"Same thing on your baked potato?"

"With a little black pepper."

"Me, too," he said. "You see, we have more in common than either of us imagined."

Amie laughed, and the roguish gleam in his eyes set her a'tingle.

"How's the wine?" he asked when she took a small sip.

"I like it. It's very delicate. I wish I could tell

you about its bouquet, but I may as well admit that I have only two ways of judging wine. If it tastes like vinegar, I know I don't like it. And if it's too sweet, it makes me sick. The only way I keep from making disastrous mistakes is to go to the wine shop, tell them what I'm serving, and ask them to choose something for me."

His smile made his eyes a warm, liquid blue, and she could see tiny flickering sparks she thought must be reflected candlelight.

Conversation was pleasant while they ate. And once, when Amie got up to get a glass of water, she spied Stranger lying peacefully beside Buck's chair, his head resting on one of his master's feet. "Stranger must miss you when you go traipsing around the world," she said, smiling when one pointed, shaggy ear lifted at the sound of his name.

"He and Luke get along fine," Buck said, reaching down to nuzzle the dog between his ears. "Luke has a little cabin down by the creek, but when I'm gone he stays here in the house so he and Stranger can look after things."

"You spend a lot of time in Peru?" she asked, remembering what Tom had told her.

"Yes, I go down as often as I can."

"You must have friends there." When the corners of his mouth tilted upward, she wanted to bite her tongue for being so obvious.

"One or two." He snuffed out the candles and reached for Amie's hand. "We'll have dessert later in front of the fire. Come on, I want to show you something."

They passed through the room Amie thought of as the gallery, where she noticed the fire that crackled in the huge fireplace. "Luke came in while we were having dinner," Buck explained. "He likes to do things around the house. I guess I'm the nearest thing to a family he has."

Amie smiled but said nothing. So Stranger was not the only one who'd been given a home. Could Buck Cameron be a fake? Was there a side to him that few suspected?

She'd been waiting for just the right time to ask him about the piece of property she'd been investigating, but even during dinner she hadn't been able to bring herself to mention it. This would probably be the best chance she'd have tonight, but the evening was so perfect she didn't want to spoil it by bringing up business, especially when she knew they'd get into an argument if he gave her a hard time.

With her hand held tightly in his, Buck led her to a large, softly lit area she knew immediately was his bedroom. Straight from the Arabian Nights, it was done in soft, pale beiges with great splashes of white. And in the very center of the room was a large, square platform covered with silk pillows of every color in the rainbow—brilliant peacock blues and greens, ruby reds, the softest pinks, purple, pale gold, and beneath them was a heavy, silk damask spread of desert sand. There was something incongruous about the room and Amie's conception of the man who occupied it, but it took her a minute to realize what it was.

She had fully expected to see a fur coverlet on his bed, and its absence both surprised and pleased her. She hadn't seen a skin anywhere in the house, nor any evidence of the taxidermy she'd so dreaded. Nowhere had she seen a single hunting trophy.

"It's a beautiful room, Buck," she said sincerely.

"This is what I want to show you," he said, tugging at her hand. "It's my favorite part of the house. In fact, of all the things I have, it's my favorite."

Clearly, he was leading her toward the bed. His favorite part of the house? Did it vibrate, have music piped through the mattress? Did he push some hidden little button that released a gaseous aphrodisiac? Surely, he didn't think he needed help along that line. All he had to do was touch her to make her go all melty inside, and she imagined any other woman would feel the same.

"You're going to love this," he said, kicking off his loafers. Sweeping her into his arms, he placed her in the middle of the enormous bed, then stretched out beside her.

"Now what?" Amie asked, unable to suppress her smile. He seemed far more like a little boy now than the lover she suspected him to be.

"Close your eyes and don't open them until I tell you," he instructed.

"Ha! You think I'm as crazy as you are? This bed does something weird, doesn't it?"

"A little faith, darlin'," he said with an enormous grin. "Now trust me and close your eyes."

Well, why not? Amie asked herself as she obediently did as he told her. When she shivered with anticipation, she heard his sensual laughter, soft and evocative, and thoughts of chains and feathers flitted through her mind . . . her deranged mind, she told herself.

Then, while entertaining visions that made her cheeks flush, she heard a noise, a sliding sound that came from somewhere above them. She lay very still, her breath bated, and then she felt his hand touch hers lightly, so lightly she could barely feel his fingertips.

Suddenly, magically, there was only a stillness. Amie felt suspended, not floating exactly, but weightless. Miraculously, she was no longer confined to a limiting body, but was a living part of something vast, wondrous, infinite. She could no longer hear herself breathe, could no longer feel a heartbeat—nor did she feel the need for either. What was he doing?

Buck's voice seemed to come from another dimension when she heard him whisper, "Now. Open your eyes."

The sound of Amie's gasp was magnified by the stillness that surrounded them. Instinctively, her fingers threaded through Buck's. The room was in total darkness. Or it would have been, she thought, if it existed. Above them, the ceiling had opened and the sky seemed close enough to touch. No, closer. She was part of the sky. Stars swirled around her; she was the mist that hovered about the moon, the whisper of the night; she was all and she was everything.

Buck's hand tightened, and its pressure became her only touchstone to reality. "Hold on," he said, and his voice, too, was a part of her.

"My God, what is it?" she asked, squeezing his hand.

"My pleasure dome." His voice was soft, deep, and mesmerizing. The room began to glow with a soft, fragile light. She felt as if they were one with infinity.

Still suspended, the aura of light spread through the room, making her aware of her own self—aware with an intensity she'd never before imagined.

A smile began slowly, somewhere deep inside her,

and gradually found its way to her lips. She was reminded of the sounds of the ocean, whispers of the night, sounds that seeped through her mind and out her pores and drew her, making her a part of the sound. Yet her thoughts were not muddled. They were crystal clear. She was in another dimension where only she and Buck existed in vast and unbelievably wondrous time and space.

"I've never shared this with anyone else," Buck said softly. "It's so special, I've kept it to myself."

"Surely you don't expect me to believe you've never had another woman in your bed."

He raised himself on his elbow and his eyes danced in the soft glow of the room as he leaned over her, blocking out the heavens and giving her an even better view of paradise. "One of these days, or nights," he said suggestively, "you'll learn that when I tell you something, it's the truth. I didn't say I've never brought another woman to the house, Amie, only that one's never been in this room."

Her heart constricted and she lowered her lashes. Why was he telling her this? Why was he confusing her by arousing thoughts and feelings she knew were better denied? Seducing her, or letting himself be seduced, was one thing. Letting her believe it could be more was another.

The only relationship she could expect, or want, from Buck was purely physical and she knew it. There could be nothing more. She'd vowed that she'd never set herself up for another fall. So why play with deeper, more volatile emotions?

Even so, she was glad he'd never had another woman here.

"Could I dare hope, darlin'," he said lazily, teasingly, "that you could be the least bit jealous?"

"Don't be ridiculous!"

"Look here, Amie love." With one finger, he lifted her chin. Their eyes met and without warning he pressed his lips to hers. The rush of response she felt was more awesome than touching the stars had been. She pressed herself hard against the silk damask coverlet. The heavens spun around her. She reached for an anchor and felt the hard, straining muscles in Buck's shoulders. Sliding her hands down his back, she found the edge of his shirt, then flattened her palms beneath it, against his bare skin. He trembled.

Buck's lips moved hungrily, persuasively against hers. His hands made a tortuous journey over the curves of her body, burning their imprint wherever they touched. She sucked in her breath when his tightly clad legs captured the lower part of her.

Spasms of desire shot through Buck, engorging his manhood. She was so incredibly soft, so pliant, so yielding, he couldn't control his body's response. A sweet, drugging hunger filled him with an unfamiliar ache. It was passion, yes, but it was more. The feeling was all mixed up with Amie and with the restlessness, the longing he often felt that he'd never been able to completely understand. He wondered if he were at the brink of discovery.

Fear stung his mind—a warning he knew he couldn't ignore. He knew now what was different about Amie. He supposed he'd known all along. She was not a woman you took for a night and then told good-bye, knowing that if you saw her again it would be fine; and if you didn't, no harm would be done. That's how it had been with other women. But not with Amie. And it was that difference that threatened him.

Run, his mind commanded. *Protect yourself. Escape.* It was the law of the jungle, and he had learned to live by it.

He shifted his body, felt the soft swell of her breasts press against his chest, and he wanted to touch their softness with his hands, with his mouth. He wanted to take her taut nipples between his lips, feel the sweet mound of her femininity, bury himself in its warm, dark center.

Beneath Buck's shirt, Amie's hands pressed against his bare back; the firm curve of her thigh pressed upward between his legs. He thought how the heat between her legs could burn away his misgivings—for now. "Now," he whispered, filling her mouth with his hot breath.

In the stillness created by the white noise from the stereo, he heard her speak his name. "Yes, darlin', what is it?"

Her head was spinning and she was soaring again, only this time the sensation was altogether different. With sudden, terrifying insight, she knew she wanted Buck more than anything she'd ever wanted. She wanted to touch him, touch him everywhere, and wanted him to touch her. And more. She wanted to be closer to him, much closer. She wanted him inside her. She was losing control, not only of her body but her mind, as well.

"I wonder if I haven't been high enough for one night," she said in a breathless, half whisper.

His teeth tugged gently at her full bottom lip. "Ah, Amie," he whispered. "We've only begun to soar." Catching her mouth fiercely with his own, his tongue thrust deeply, possessively.

Amie's back arched, but even as she drew him to

her she twisted her head to the side. "No, please, no," she murmured.

Buck threw himself backward against the sea of pillows, running his fingers through his damp hair. He heard her breath catch in a near sob.

He ached to hold her, but he knew his limits. And now he knew Amie's. If he touched her now, there would be no return for either of them . . . and she had said no.

But *why*, damn it? Why did she resist when he knew she wanted him? In that contradictory mind of hers, did she suspect, as did he, that they were tempting a situation neither was prepared to see to its completion? Was Amie as wary as he of becoming too involved?

For the first time in his life, he was afraid of the consequences of making love to a woman. *Damn.* He touched the controls of the stereo and the room swelled with the ethereal sound of glacier music. *Damn,* he thought again.

He felt the soft touch of Amie's hand on his arm and heard her short, hard breath that echoed his own misery.

"Darlin'," he said. "Let's get the hell out of here. That is, unless . . ."

She wanted him so much it hurt when she laughed. "With all your good intentions, you couldn't resist one more dare, could you?"

"I wanted to make sure you hadn't changed your mind, that's all," he replied teasingly, touching a switch that flooded the room with light. At the same time Amie heard the panels in the ceiling slide together.

Buck grinned, wiped the sweat from his brow, and gave her an affectionate pop on her rear. "Believe me, it was not a dare. You know as well as I that sooner or later I'm going to make love to you, Amie.'' His grin spread over his face and in that lazy voice that did crazy things to her insides, he said, ''I guess I knew that when I heard you tell Tom Delahunt you were surprised I was not wearing boots with spurs.''

''You were eavesdropping!'' She grabbed a blue silk pillow and whammed him on the shoulder.

''Huh-uh. I was re-writing the script,'' he said with a gleam in his eyes, deflecting a lavender pillow with his forearm.

''You were showing off, that's what you were doing! You're an exhibitionist or you wouldn't have gone dressed like that.'' The yellow pillow caught him on his chest. The rose one had tassles, and it was too tempting to let go of them, so she bounced it rapidly off first his head and then his arms and shoulders. She didn't notice that he was not fighting back, only laughing, protecting himself. Caught in the spirit of her successful attack, she landed astride him, tumbling forward as he fell backward.

''That's enough!'' he said, capturing her arms.

How easily his superior strength immobilized her. Staring into his eyes, she saw how dark and heated they'd become. His chest rose, then lowered as he exhaled with a deep, shuddering sigh.

''You haven't told me about your pleasure dome,'' she said, feeling a moment's awkwardness, especially in the position she was in.

''It's my secret extravagance,'' he said, rolling onto his side and placing her beside him. His breath was still ragged, but with a calming gesture he laid his hand in the valley at her waist. ''The idea came to me one night in Peru. I had decided not to go into the village, but to spend the night in my sleeping bag.

"I've been there so often during the past ten years, I don't use a guide anymore. So there I was, lying on my back, staring at the stars that seemed so close. I wondered how I was going to make myself stick to my plan to leave the next day. I'd been gone three weeks, and it was during a time when Cameron was doing a lot of expanding, and I knew I couldn't neglect my responsibilities to the family any longer.

"I decided that since I couldn't spend all my time on a mountaintop," he said, "I'd find a way to bring the stars to me. When I got back to Charlotte I called a friend of mine in Chapel Hill who works closely with the planetarium there. He made a few calls of his own and got in touch with an astronomer who contacted a man on the west coast whose company refracts lenses for telescopes. A little over a year and a small fortune later, and *voilá,* my pleasure dome."

"It's a telescope?" Amie asked with astonishment. "It isn't an illusion, but the real thing?"

Buck's laughter was pleasure-filled. "It's one of the most powerful telescopes in the country—certainly the largest," he said, drawing a finger from her forehead down the bridge of her nose, her lips, throat, and into the valley between her breasts, chuckling when she shivered with sensuous delight. "If I can't have the real thing, darlin'," he said in that husky, sexy voice of his, "then I'll damned well do without."

"And you don't do that very often, do you?" she asked quietly.

"Do without?" His grin was purely wicked. "No, I'm willing to admit, I don't often do that." Then he laughed, letting his hand wander downward to knead half-circles into her belly. "You know the old saying, sweet Amie. Where there's a will, there's a way."

Where there's a will, she thought, rolling from beneath his touch. When he made no attempt to stop her, she was a bit surprised.

"Are you ready for dessert?" he asked, stunning her with so simple a question.

"I don't think so," she replied. "I think we'd better think about getting me home."

"You're probably right," Buck agreed, sliding off the bed to stand beside her. His eyes lightened when his smile reached them. "It's going to take more than the deli's chocolate mousse to sate our appetites, darlin'. And tonight I think we're both too anxious to come to proper terms with that."

"*Anxious?* What do you *mean, anxious?*"

The sound of his mocking laughter made her sudden urge to kick him so strong she could barely restrain her foot.

"So that's what you do when you're frustrated, is it? Speak with emphasis—almost in italics?"

"You're . . . I've never . . . you can be so *aggravating,*" she sputtered.

"Can you wait long enough for me to let Stranger go out?"

He asked with a calmness that nearly made her choke. How could he be so nonchalant about the whole thing? All evening she'd been wrestling with one of life's crises. And now that he'd told her she was too anxious to set her emotions straight, putting out his dog was suddenly his top priority?

"We usually take a walk together about this time," Buck said, "but he won't take long if he goes out alone."

They reached the kitchen and Stranger was waiting underneath the table. His ears perked up and his bushy tail began to wag. "I have a better idea," Buck said. "It would be a shame for him to miss his walk tonight. When I'm not here, Luke always goes with him. Why don't you come along? The night air and a brisk walk might be good for what ails us."

Amie looked reluctantly from Buck to Stranger, who was putting one paw in front of the other, sliding forward from beneath the table. So why should the poor dog suffer just because she was in misery? And especially when she'd had her chance and blew it, all because of the crazy, mixed-up notions playing havoc with her mind. A good, brisk walk might put a better perspective on the whole evening.

They walked across the wide stretch of lawn to the edge of the wood, then rounded the top of the hill and headed toward the valley below. Stranger ran in and out of the wood, disappearing for long stretches of time. He'd run back to sniff at their ankles, to have his shaggy mane tousled by his master, and then run away again to chase a real or imaginary rabbit.

For the most part, Buck and Amie walked in silence—sometimes comfortable silence, sometimes electrified when their shoulders would touch, or their hands would brush as they swung them in cadence with their footsteps.

"Feel better now?" he asked when he locked the door after putting Stranger back inside the house.

"It was a nice walk. I enjoyed it," she replied.

Inside the car, silence fell warm and easy. When they did talk, it was only light and chatty conversation. Buck asked about Tom and Millie; Amie asked about Cameron, Inc. and was fascinated to hear that Buck's great-grandfather had started the business with one general store at the turn of the century. Buck mentioned Lizbeth, saying he'd like to meet her, and then surprised Amie by asking, "How do you get along with Marsha Dellinger?"

Ah, yes. Marsha. And what a perfect opening. "Better than you, from what I've gathered."

His expression didn't change. "What does that mean?" he asked.

"We had a little flare-up at the office. It's obvious she thinks you're a louse."

There was a moment's silence and she thought surely he was going to give her an explanation. When he only grunted, she didn't know whether to pry or leave it be. "I told her you aren't a louse . . . that you're a tiger cat."

"And you're right," he said.

She decided she'd been right about not prying, but knew that one day soon her curiosity would get the best of her.

At her door, Buck touched her cheek lightly with his hand.

"If you don't want to come with me to the race next weekend, I don't know when I'll see you again," he said. "When I'm not having board meetings during the week, I'll be making short trips out of town to check on some financing we're lining up for a new project we're involved in."

Amie swallowed her disappointment. "Be careful," she said. "I mean, I guess you know what you're doing when you're racing those fast cars. And a special thanks for sharing your pleasure dome."

He lifted her chin and looked deeply into her eyes.

She felt her cheeks flush and put her hand to her throat. "Amie, Amie," he said softly. The sound of her name on his lips made every part of her begin to ache all over again. His eyes brightened. "I'm not going to kiss you," he said quietly, "because if I do, I won't be able to leave."

Just the thought of his mouth on hers made her lips throb. "I . . ."

She was about to say she wished he wouldn't leave, but before she could get the words out he said, "Good night, Amie."

For one heart-stopping moment their eyes held, sent messages of desire, confusion, despair. Amie turned to insert her key in the lock. Before she heard its click, she heard Buck's retreating footsteps. As much as she was tempted, she didn't look back.

SEVEN

Buck paced back and forth in his hotel room at Daytona. He'd called Amie's private extension at the office, but she hadn't answered. Then he tried her apartment with no better luck. Now, hours later when she should be home feeding her cats, she still didn't answer. Where could she be?

When he left for the race in Daytona, he hadn't made up his mind. But now he knew he wanted to take Amie to his parents' anniversary dinner. If he waited any longer to tell her, she'd think it was a last minute decision and, knowing Amie, she wouldn't be too happy with that. He chuckled to himself. Amie Phillips was some kind of woman. His dad was going to love her.

Maybe her mother or Marsha would know her whereabouts. Amie might not like it if he called her mother, and he knew damned well Marsha wouldn't like it if he called her. But what the hell. It wouldn't kill Marsha to have one short conversation with him. Shaking his head, he wondered if she'd ever stop blaming him for what happened to her husband.

He dialed information, but after the operator gave him Marsha's number, he almost changed his mind. Then he decided it was worth being called a few choice names to find out where Amie was. When Marsha answered, he was stunned to find her so accommodating.

"Amie left early today, Buck," she said. "I think she was going out of town."

"Out of town? Where out of town?"

"She didn't tell me. I'm not even sure who she was going with."

"She didn't go alone?"

"Why on earth would she do that? What kind of fun would that be?"

Buck thanked her, then almost knocked the phone off the wall when he slammed the receiver down.

So, she went to have fun, did she? Fun. What the hell did that mean? Whatever, he intended to find out.

"So, what was it like?" Millie wanted to know the minute she and Amie settled themselves in the Delahunts' den. "I've heard all kinds of stories about Buck Cameron's lair, and I've been dying to hear about it firsthand."

Amie almost wished she hadn't told Millie that she'd gone to Buck's home. It was weird, but she didn't want to talk about it. "It's just a house, Millie," she said. "As he said, he isn't into cooking in a big way, so we had steaks and a salad, then listened to some music."

"Um-hmmm. You know what it means when you lie to your best friend, don't you?" Millie asked with a you-know-I-don't-believe-a-word-you're-saying look.

Amie laughed. "No, what does it mean, know-it-all?"

"It means you slept with the guy and don't want to tell me about it."

"I did not!"

Millie shot out to the edge of the sofa. "Don't give me that, Amie Phillips. You can leave out the bumps and the grinds. That's not the part I'm interested in. I want to know if his bedroom's really as decadent as they say."

Amie felt her dander rise. "As *who* says?"

"Aha!" Millie shouted, pointing her finger at Amie. "You *did* sleep with him or you wouldn't be so jealous."

"Jealous? Who says I'm jealous?"

"*Who says his bedroom is decadent?* That's what you wanted to know, Amie. Quick as a reflex. So, I say you're jealous."

"Curious, that's all."

Millie settled back on the sofa and gave Amie an enigmatic smile. "I'm only pulling your leg. But I'll tell you one thing. If that Casanova hurts you, I'll sic Tom on him."

"He can't hurt me if I don't let him," Amie said, wishing she felt as confident as she sounded. "You have to be vulnerable to get hurt."

"You're a real fraud, do you know that?" Before Amie could reply, Millie smiled and asked, "*Did* you make love? Does he do it the same way the rest of us do? Tell me!"

Amie's face flushed and she wanted to strangle Millie. "His bedroom is every bit as decadent as they say . . . whoever *they* are . . . and no, we did not make love, so I don't know what his technique is. I imagine he has the same plumbing Tom and every other man has, so I don't know how he could do it any differently from the way they do. If I find out, I'll let you know."

Millie groaned loudly. "Do you mean to tell me you made it to the bedroom and nothing happened? What makes me believe you're telling me the truth? Good grief, Amie. If you got that far, how could you pass up the chance to really get to . . . well, you know?"

"Millie! You make it sound as if he's kinky or something."

"Maybe not that, but any woman in her right mind can see the devil in those blue eyes of his. I'll bet they've done more than melt cold hearts."

"And all this time you've been warning me against him," Amie reminded her.

"I didn't lead you to the trough, remember? Once you're there, though, you may as well satisfy your thirst."

"Ummm. He does have beautiful eyes, doesn't he?" Amie said dreamily.

"If that's all you've noticed, then I guess you're pretty safe," Millie said with a chuckle and a wicked little wink. "But you know I'm only kidding. You be careful of him, unless you can swim the Channel and scale Mount Everest without benefit of water wings or a helicopter."

"Somehow, I get the feeling he doesn't give a woman more than one chance—or a man or beast either, for that matter," Amie said soulfully. "He hasn't called once since then."

Millie eyed her thoughtfully. "You sound disappointed. Are you?"

"Yes, if you want the truth. There's something about him, Millie . . . something different. Oh, I don't know. Maybe all I want is some excitement in my life. Only . . ."

"There are plenty of good men around just twitching to give excitement, honey. I've been telling you that for ages. But Buck Cameron isn't any ole man. I'm not sure he'd make a good playmate, if you know what I mean."

"I'm not so sure about that," said Amie. "Sometimes I think that's all he ever wants to be—a playmate. But yes, I do know what you mean," she agreed. "He could probably be rough at his games."

"You'd better believe it. I hear that man plays hardball and when you take your chances on the court with him, you'd best have a first-aid kit waiting in the stands."

Driving home, Amie decided that maybe she was naive, after all. Millie's opinion of Buck wasn't much different from Marsha's. But they didn't know him the way she did.

And what makes you think you know him? she asked herself.

"Amie?" Lizbeth asked when her daughter answered the phone.

"I was going to call you tomorrow, Mother, when the rates are lower."

"It's well past five," her mother said, "and it's Friday. It doesn't cost any more to call now that it would tomorrow."

"Is everything all right?"

"That's what I called to ask you," Lizbeth informed her. "Who's Buck Cameron?"

"What do you know about *him?*"

"Nothing! That's why I'm asking."

"Lord, Mother, you are logical if nothing else, aren't you?"

"What do you mean, if nothing else? I'm the only mother you have, Amie Phillips, and that makes me something. You'd best not forget that, either."

"I doubt you'll give me the opportunity, Mother."

"I didn't call to hear any of your sass, young woman."

"I'm sorry, Mother. You know I love you."

Lizbeth made a coughing sound. "Sweet talking me won't make me forget why I called. I want to know why some man calling himself Buck Cameron would call me."

"I'd like to know that, too, Mother. When did he call?"

"About an hour ago. He said he'd been trying to get you since this afternoon. He wanted to know if you were here, and I told him I hadn't seen you if you were. Why weren't you at work this afternoon? And what man do you know well enough to give him my telephone number? What's going on, Amie, that you haven't told your mother?"

"I put an ad in the paper, Mother, that I'm sex starved and looking for a live-in. I didn't want every stud in town calling me, so I gave your number. I thought you'd do a good job of screening for me."

"Amie!"

"Don't hang up," Amie said quickly. "What else did Buck say?"

"So it's Buck, is it? Not Mr. Cameron?"

"Are you going to tell me what he said?"

"Not until you tell me where you've been and who he is."

Amie sighed and reached for her cup of tea. "All right, Mother. One, I left work early because I've been working long hours and thought I deserved an afternoon off. I spent it with Millie, went by the spa, and here I am, safe and sound. Two, Buck Cameron is an acquaintance of mine. We've been out for hotdogs once, and . . ."

"Knowing you, you'd go out with about anybody if they promised you a hotdog," Lizbeth interjected. "That doesn't tell me anything."

What could she tell her? Who, exactly, *is* Buck Cameron? And is it true? Is he no more than an acquaintance? she asked herself. If she told Lizbeth he was the only man who had ever taken her to touch the stars, she'd know she was crazy. If she told her he was the one man in the whole world she understood least and wanted to sleep with most, Lizbeth would send someone to dress her in a little white jacket.

"He's a very nice person, Mother."

"He said he was trying to find you, that's all," Lizbeth replied. "I told him I didn't know where you could be; that you never tell your mother anything."

" 'Bye, Mother. I love you."

"Marsha!" she muttered on her way to the kitchen. She wadded her napkin and threw it into the wastebasket with all her might, then was angry when it floated to the bottom and didn't make a noise. If Buck called the office, why didn't Marsha tell him she was at Millie's? She knew she'd told Marsha where she'd be, just in case Whitney Crawford called. It just went to show how much attention Marsha paid to anything Amie said.

Buck would be driving in that awful race tomorrow, and she could have wished him luck. She remembered telling him that her mother lived in Pinehurst, so he must have gotten the number from directory assistance. Whatever he wanted to tell her must have been important, or he wouldn't have gone to that much trouble to find her. She chuckled. That was one conversation she was glad she hadn't heard. She did so hope Lizbeth hadn't put him through the third degree.

When the phone rang she was in such a tizzy trying to get to it before the caller hung up, she nearly stumbled over her own feet.

"Ms. Phillips?"

Her heart plummeted. She'd been so certain it would be Buck. "Yes?"

"This is Whitney Crawford with the planning commission," he said. "Charlie Overcash was in my office this week telling me about your thoughts on our inner-city housing problem."

Amie's spirits soared. Surely Crawford wouldn't be calling her if not with good news.

"Did he tell you about the tract of land I feel would be pivotal to my proposal?"

"In fact, that's what I'm calling about," Whitney Crawford said. "There have been a lot of complaints recently about street people loitering downtown. It hurts business, you know. Your plan could be just the thing to solve this problem. It's very innovative, and we're impressed by the work you've done on it. So much so, we've checked out that piece of property."

"That's wonderful," Amie said. "You know, then, that it belongs to McCauley Real Estate and to the Camerons."

"Don't get your hopes up, Ms. Phillips," Crawford warned. "I've talked with McCauley and they're willing to sell. We suggested a little incentive, of course. With the right deal, McCauley could likely do the work. We're afraid the hitch could be the Camerons, though. You see, they were against a similar proposal some time back, and they didn't even own the land in question. I don't know how they'll feel about this, considering they've talked to McCauley about putting a high-rise office building there."

"But it's so close to the Fourth Ward, and that whole area is residential."

"True enough. But that's part of the consideration, you see. Close as it is to both the Fourth and Second Wards, this particular property is in the downtown area and the zoning is not residential."

"But there isn't too much involved in changing it, is there?" Amie asked.

Crawford chuckled. "I like your enthusiasm, Amie, but the main hurdle to get over here is the Cameron family. You know Buck pretty well, don't you?"

Incredible, Amie thought. In a city the size of Charlotte gossip seemed to travel as fast as it did in a small town. "You could say we're on speaking terms."

"Yes, well, you apparently did a fine job convincing both the Apartment Association and the Uptown Development Corporation that this plan of yours is workable. I wondered if you might not be better at enticing the Camerons than even McCauley could possibly be. You see, as a business proposition, I don't think low-income housing is high on most people's list, and especially not for someone who already opposes bringing it downtown. Now, if you could soften Buck up a little, we could possibly take it from there."

She had every intention of talking to Buck about this property, but Whitney Crawford's suggestion somehow offended her. She knew it was ridiculous to feel this way, but she couldn't help it. "I don't know, Mr. Crawford," she said hesitantly.

It was the *softening up* part, she decided. That was not her intention at all. She'd felt all along that if she explained her plan to Buck he would see its merit. She wasn't above doing a little persuading, but she intended to use logic and reason, not her feminine wiles. That was the only way she'd feel right about it.

"It's only a suggestion," Crawford said. "The Camerons are generous when it comes to civic affairs, but they draw the line where business is concerned. Low-income housing will never turn the profit that a high-rise office building will."

"Let me think about it," Amie said.

"Well, let me know how it goes. There's no point in talking finances until we know if the property can be made available. It's a good time for something like this, because I understand that there are big chunks of money in Washington right now for low-income housing, and our representatives might be able to swing some our way."

Amie promised to get in touch with Crawford and let him know if she talked with Buck about it. While she'd had every intention of explaining her plan to Buck, she tried to convince herself that Crawford's suggestion should have no bearing on how she felt about it. But it did. If Buck thought she was collaborating with the Planning Commission, she could easily see him refusing to cooperate. If he had other plans for that property, as Crawford indicated, she doubted he could be persuaded to change his mind. Crawford was right. Buck was out to turn a profit.

She wished now Crawford had waited until Monday and called her at her office. The possibility of her plan's failing would hang over her all weekend.

When the phone rang again, her voice didn't have its usual cheerful tone when she answered.

"Don't you ever tell your mother where to find you?"

Buck's voice cleared her mind as sweetly as a

summer rain makes a dusty landscape sparkle. Laughter bubbled up and out as she curled her feet beneath her on the sofa and waited to hear him speak again.

"What's so damned funny?" he asked. "Do you know what I've been through trying to find you?"

Realizing she'd been worried about him driving in that race, and that part of her euphoria came from knowing he was all right, her voice was almost musical. "I thought you said my laughter made you feel warm inside," she teased, straightening her legs and stretching her toes. When she heard him chuckle, her toes curled tightly.

"I almost didn't call back," he said. "Marsha told me you'd gone away for the weekend . . . and not alone," he said pointedly. "But the more I thought about it, and especially after I talked to Lizbeth, the less I trusted what Marsha had said. So, I decided to give it one more try."

"Hold it. Marsha told you *what?*"

"Forget it," Buck said. "She likes to sabotage me, but this time it didn't work."

At this point, Amie was past worrying about whether he'd think she was prying or not. "What is it with you and Marsha, Buck? This thing keeps coming up, and now she's involved me. What is it with you two?"

"Not now, darlin'. I'll explain it later when we have time to talk. Right now, it's you I want to talk about. Do you know you're the only woman I've ever worried about, with the exception of my own mother?" he asked gruffly. "I don't know what it is about you, Amie. You must have gotten more than your share of your mother's genes."

"Are you saying my mother's batty?"

"A little bit," he said with a deep chuckle.

Amie laughed. "Yeah, you're right. We share the same belfry, I guess. She said you called her."

"You've talked with Lizbeth?"

"No, I listened while she talked to me. I hope you still have ears."

There was a sudden blast of music in the background. "I only have a minute," Buck said. "Some of the guys are getting together tonight and the only time I see most of them is when I race with them. I called because Sunday is my parents' anniversary and the family's getting together to help them celebrate. I'll probably stay here tomorrow night. My return ticket's for Sunday, but I thought this would be a good time for you to meet my folks. Is eight o'clock okay?"

Meet his family? "Won't you be tired when you get home? I'd think you'd enjoy simply relaxing with your family."

She didn't need an imagination to see the grin on his face when he spoke. "So far, Amie love, I haven't needed much energy when we've been together. I could burn more calories flat on my back. Are you trying to tell me something, perchance?"

Her stomach did a fair imitation of an eggbeater. "Only that you're not funny. Ha–ha funny, I mean." She heard someone calling his name in the background, and then laughter—female laughter.

"I've got to go now, darlin'. I'll see you Sunday around eight."

For what seemed an eternity, Amie stood staring at the phone in her hand. It was a foregone conclusion that she and Buck had little in common. When it came to women, he was into pluralism. And she was, on a serious plane, a one-man woman. She was an Independent, who leaned heavily toward the left, and he was a dyed-in-the-wool conservative. He was a free spirit, taking off to far parts of the world on a whim. She was a homebody, though she never talked about it, and liked sitting in front of a fire with a good book and classical jazz in the background.

The only thing left was an over-powering sexual attraction, and if she kept seeing him, she knew exactly where it would lead. And the way she felt right now, it couldn't happen soon enough. Looking at it in this light, there was only one plausible consequence to consider. She already knew the effect his kisses had on her. If they made love, would she be able to survive it?

"That," she said, pointing her finger at Charlie, "is the real question, isn't it, boy?"

It rained during the night, and Saturday morning was as bright as a wash hung on the line to dry. Amie aired her apartment, then drove to Pinehurst. So she wouldn't have to answer too many questions about Buck—questions for which she felt she had no adequate answers to give Lizbeth—she took her mother to lunch at The Inn and then to the grocery store.

It was almost six when Amie exited I–85, and with heavy traffic, another thirty minutes before she pulled into her drive. She hurried inside and turned on the television, hoping to catch the sports on the news. The meteorologist was in the middle of the weather report, which always came at the end of the program, so she knew she'd have to wait until eleven o'clock to see how Buck had fared in the race.

She fed the cats, took a shower, and did her hair. Exhausted from her day of traveling to Pinehurst and back, she took a paperback and climbed into bed. When Brigette's cold nose woke her, it was Sunday morning.

Still in her pajamas, she ran outside to get the morning paper. Thumbing to the sports section, she scanned the page that covered the race. Buck had come in third. That was phenomenal, she thought, considering the fact that racing was only one of his many avocations. She hoped he was not disappointed.

Almost a third of the page was given to a photograph of the winner holding his trophy and receiving his six-figure share of the pot. The usual bevy of bathing beauties stood in the background, surrendering the spotlight to the winning driver and his wife.

Amie turned the page to see if there was anything else about the race, or if Buck's name was mentioned again anywhere. "Well, would you look at that!" she said to Brigette.

The black-and-white photograph at the top of the page might just as well have been in living color for all its impact. "Have you ever heard the expression, sparks were flying, Brigette? If you want to see a perfect example of what it means, take a *good* look at *that!*"

Brigette made a yowling sound and leapt to the top of the kitchen door. "That's exactly how I feel," Amie mumbled as she stared at the voluptuous blonde who commanded more attention than the trophy Buck held in the crook of one arm.

It was enough that he was kissing her. Did he have to get caught by a photographer in such a lewd pose? Or didn't he care if the whole world saw him pressed so close to that woman you couldn't tell them from Siamese twins?

So he stayed over to party with the guys, did he? "Damn him," she screamed. Wishing it were Buck's head, she crushed the paper between both hands and flung it across the room, retrieved it, threw it on the floor, and stamped on it. Snatching the paper from the floor, she ran to the laundry room and placed it beneath the litter box.

All day she fumed, vacillating between going and not going to Buck's parents' anniversary dinner. By four o'clock she'd exhausted every reason, pro and con. As little as she knew about racing, she did know there were always a Miss Watermelon, a Miss Peach, and a Miss Whoever waiting to pose with the winners. A publicity gimmick. She knew that. A pro. But why couldn't Buck have drawn Miss Watermelon instead of a *Playboy* centerfold? Definitely a con.

A pro was the fact that she didn't want to be rude to his parents if they were expecting her. They couldn't help it if they had a womanizing hyena for a son.

Not once did she admit to herself that hyena or not, he'd effectively done what she'd sworn he'd never do—captured her thoughts and confused her emotions. Neither a pro nor a con.

Around five o'clock she showered, wrapped herself in a big terry towel, and went to her bedroom. Brigette came inside and meowed.

"It's a narrow margin," Amie said to the cat, "but the pros seem to have it."

EIGHT

Amie tossed her towel across the bed and reached for a bottle of body lotion on her vanity. The doorbell chose that moment to ring.

She glanced at the small travel clock on her bedside table. It was barely six. The bell rang a second time. Slipping into a short cotton robe, she hurried to answer it.

Like a panther, Buck paced the small front porch. When the door opened, he pivoted. "What were you . . . Oh, you were taking a bath."

Instantly, Amie knew she was glad the pros won out. "I just finished," she said, realizing her skin was still damp and flushed. "It's only six o'clock." Stepping back for him to push past her, she added, "I haven't begun to dress."

"Close the door, Amie. Come here. God, I couldn't wait to hold you." He drew her forcefully into his arms. "I'm disappointed I missed your bath. I'd like to see you all warm and soft in a cloud of bubbles. I'd be tempted to climb in with you, help bathe you."

Something primal surged inside her that made her arch against him.

He made a growling sound, much the way she imagined one of the big cats she'd seen in his photographs would. His hands slipped beneath her robe, fingering, touching, caressing as he spoke. Amie rose on tiptoe to twine her arms around him.

"It's so good to see you," he said, "to hold you like this."

Then he kissed her, covering her mouth with his own, thrusting his tongue between her parted lips, probing inside until her breath quickened and her heart pounded against his chest. She strained against him, an effort to assuage the aching hunger between her legs.

"I want you, Amie," he said gruffly. "I can't tell you how much, but I do intend to show you. This time you're not running, and neither am I."

"Running?"

"We've both been afraid," Buck said. "I know you have, and that's why I haven't pushed. I didn't want you with reservations. Mine or yours. And you had to want me as much as I want you . . . all of you . . . with no holding back."

His hands were playing havoc with her senses, touching her everywhere, holding, squeezing. "We don't understand what's happening between us, and that's what scares us. But I've reached the point where I don't even care what it is. All I know is that I want you. Want you . . ." Hungrily, his mouth took hers again.

It was a harsh, yet gentle kiss, plundering, taking, yet filling, giving. Amie's arms held him, her mouth clung to his, her fingers dug into the hard muscles of his shoulders and she moaned her pleasure, her need, her own want.

Mindless, she left his words to hover in the back of her consciousness. She would translate them later. Now there was only feeling and it was enough.

His hands roamed the length of her from her thick, tangled hair, down her neck, over her shoulders, and farther downward where he dug his fingers into the firm flesh and pulled her roughly against him.

Barely aware of their passage to the bedroom, she gave no thought to the fact that he cast aside her robe somewhere along the way. He dropped his own clothes beside her bed while his eyes traveled over her—caressing, heating—and she reached for him even before he touched her and found her hot and moist, ready for him.

"Hold me," he said as he lowered himself beside her. "Put your arms around me, Amie. Yes, like this." He tangled a hand in her hair and began to kiss her while he touched her breasts, smoothed over her belly, let his fingers tease the curling vee of auburn hair to tantalize her soft, moist, sensitive folds of flesh.

"Don't tighten up, darling," he whispered, pressing small, tender kisses along the length of her neck. "That's it, open for me, Amie, love. Let me show you how good we can be together."

Amie's head stopped thrashing on the pillow. Her shoulders raised off the bed and her fingers dug into him as she choked back a sob of pure pleasure. His fingers drove deeply into her softness and he pushed her back down with the pressure of his mouth on her engorged breasts. His fingers explored, then began a steady, tortuous rhythm while his mouth feasted first on one breast and then the other. When she could stand it no longer without shattering, she cried out to him. "I want you, Buck. You. You. *You.*"

"Do you, darling? Is this what you want?"

Hard and pulsing, he touched his powerful erection to the place where his hand had been.

"Yes!" Amie arched, forcing him to enter her, but he withdrew.

Her head careened backward, thrusting her breasts toward him and her nipples brushed against the crisp hair on his chest. She drew his tongue between her teeth, deep inside her mouth, wrapped her legs around him, her heels on his buttocks, and pressed downward, trying to force him inside her again. His body moved beneath her hands, hot and sweaty. Her soft, husky voice began to chant his name.

Gasping, Buck raised himself over her. His features were tightly drawn, his body taut, his eyes clouded. "Go ahead, darling," he rasped. "Take what you want."

Her hand slid between them. Buck shuddered, calling out her name when her fingers closed around him.

For just an instant she held him. She wanted to feel this part of him, so alive, pulsing against her hand. But it was not enough. She positioned him, but before she could raise her hips, he drove inside her.

This time he didn't tease. He thrust inside her, driving deep, deeper. Again and again he thrust, and Amie rose to meet him, born to his rhythm, lost to the exquisite pleasure that mounted feverishly, spiralled through her, claimed her breath, herself. And then she exploded, shattered into myriad sparks that shot toward infinity.

Slowly, ever so slowly, she came together again to find herself held tightly, lovingly in Buck's arms. She opened her eyes to find him looking at her, looking in the strangest way. "What?" she asked on her breath.

Unsmiling, he said in a voice deliciously warm and husky, "Damned if I know what. I've never felt like that before."

Then he kissed her with an exquisite tenderness. Hot tears pushed against her lashes. Her voice trembled when she spoke. "Me, too."

While Buck showered, Amie took a quick sponge bath, then hurried to her room to dress. She didn't want to give too much thought to what had happened between them. Not yet. There would be time for that later when she was alone. *Maybe too much time,* a little voice warned before she banished it.

She settled on a simple, white wool crêpe jacket-dress. Its softly draped neckline was flattering, she thought, and she chose a wide belt of supple white leather with a gemstone buckle. The only other accessory she wore was a pair of large silver earrings she had made in a crafts class she took while she was still in Raleigh.

Her thick, chestnut hair had grown since she moved to Charlotte, and now it was a little below her shoulders. At first she pulled it back, then decided to let it hang loose and brushed it until she could see burnished highlights. She powdered the end of her nose, used a very light hand with her green eye-shadow wand, and barely touched the tips of her lashes with mascara. Her cheeks were still flushed from their lovemaking, though she never needed blush anyway. But she did touch her full lips with some coral lip gloss.

A final inspection in her full-length mirror made her feel confident she could pass the inspection of Buck's conservative family.

"You're truly beautiful, do you know that?"

In the mirror she saw Buck standing in the doorway. "I've never seen you in a suit!" she exclaimed, thinking how handsome he looked in the light wool shadow-plaid suit. The blue cotton shirt had a tiny burgundy stripe that matched his silk tie. Very much the power look, she thought. But it was the smile he was wearing that said it was Buck.

"About the only times I try to conform," he said while letting his gaze drift over her, "are on Mom's birthday and on their anniversary. I guess it's my way of paying homage to them for my being here. Anyway," he said offhandedly, "it's the same thing I was wearing when I came to your door."

Amie grinned. "But I wasn't looking at your clothes then," she said.

"No?" He began the few steps across the room. "What were you looking at?"

"You." Her grin broadened. "And I may have forgotten what you were wearing at the door, but I remember very well a certain little pink birthmark I saw when you weren't wearing anything."

"You do, huh?" His hands curved over her shoulders.

"Uh-huh. It's right on the tip of . . ." Her words were lost in his mouth when he kissed her. Briefly. Far too briefly.

"We'd better get going," he said, squeezing her arm. "My folks don't know I'm home yet and they may start dinner without us."

"You haven't called them?"

"Didn't have time. I went home from the airport, took a quick shower, then dressed and headed over here before I knew what I was doing. I came in third, by the way."

"I read the sports page this morning," Amie said. "Congratulations."

"Yeah. How 'bout that?" His attitude was casual and offhand.

A sharp pain twisted inside Amie. It was a premonition, she thought. It was a warning of what it would be like for any woman with no more sense than to fall in love with Buck Cameron. A woman like herself. Placing in the winner's circle apparently was no more or no less important to him than risking his life, and that he seemed to do on a regular and calculated basis. This time he had won, but he could as easily have been part of a tangled and twisted mass of metal on the racetrack.

"Yeah, how 'bout that?" Amie repeated as he helped her slip into her jacket. "Darth Vader thought he had it down pat, too."

Buck laughed and turned her toward him. The pleased, boyish smile on his handsome face only tightened the pain in her chest. "Don't tell me you were worried about me. Taking risks is what it's all about, Amie."

"Then break your stupid neck!" she muttered, trying to swallow the lump in her throat. She turned her head quickly so he wouldn't see the sheen of her eyes. She was as shocked by her reaction as she was angry with his. Damn it. She was over-reacting. His daredevil attitude was nothing new.

Buck took her chin firmly in his hand, forcing her to look back at him. When she lowered her lashes, he only tilted her chin upward. The position demanded that she either close her eyes, stare cross-eyed at her nose, or meet Buck's piercing blue gaze. "I worry about strays, too," she murmured, lifting her lashes courageously.

The sober look on Buck's face shook her with a new kind of pain. Dear God, she prayed silently. Why did you let me fall so hard for a man I can't begin to understand?

As quickly as he had captured her gaze, Buck released her and nodded toward her purse that was lying on the sofa. "I guess you're taking that? We'd better hurry, hon."

"We shouldn't have spent so long . . ."

"Don't say that," he said, looking deep into her eyes. "It wasn't nearly long enough."

She shook her head slightly, hoping to regain her equilibrium. She couldn't give a name to the way he looked at her. There was a teasing quality, an element of seduction, something of a dare, and tenderness all reflected in his eyes. Every nerve in her body responded and her heart got confused and thought it was supposed to be in her throat.

Her arm tingled when his hand closed around it. While she caught her breath, Buck took her key and locked the front door. He put the key back into her purse, then rushed her down the walk. Opening his car door, he helped her inside, hurried around the front, and slid in beside her. He leaned over her, again taking her chin in his hand.

"I was afraid to give you much of a kiss inside because I knew we'd never leave if I did. There's not a helluva lot we can do in the car with all our clothes on." His grin was audacious. "At least, not when we're on our way to the folks' house. That's why I hurried you. Out here you'll be safe from my marauding hands and we'll still have a few minutes before I have to share you." He chuckled softly, seductively. "You haven't sated my appetite, darlin'. I still need you. Bad."

As his mouth descended, Amie put up her hand. "Buck, I'm wearing lip gloss. I don't think . . ."

With his thumb, he gently rubbed her upper lip, letting his eyes follow the movement. "Open your mouth," he said, his voice very low. She parted her lips and his thumb rubbed from one corner of her soft, pliant bottom lip to its center, and with his forefinger, he wiped from the other corner. "Don't close your mouth. Keep it exactly the way it is," he said, lowering his face until his lips were barely an inch from hers.

She couldn't wait any longer. "Kiss me, Buck," she commanded.

And he did, and the memory of him inside her flashed through her mind in vivid color. When he lifted his mouth, they were both trembling.

"You're coming home with me when we leave the folks tonight." She looked at him helplessly. "Say it," Buck whispered.

And Amie said, "Yes. Yes, yes, yes."

The car thrust forward and into the night, its headlights throwing a long streak of light that led them onward.

When they turned onto Providence Road, Buck glanced at the clock on the dashboard. "We'll get there with a breath to spare," he said. "It's only about ten more minutes."

For some reason, Amie felt anxious about tonight. She hadn't felt like this since . . . since she was a teenager, she thought with a smile. Ridiculous. What was there to be anxious about? Determined not to think any more about meeting Buck's family, she remembered Whitney Crawford's call. "Whitney Crawford called me yesterday," she said.

"Whitney Crawford?"

"He was calling about a piece of property I've tracked down that would be perfect for a housing project I'm working on."

It always irritated her somewhat when Buck showed so little interest in her work. Even if he didn't believe in what she was doing, he could at least hear her out. When he said nothing, she continued.

"Charlotte's so short of low-income housing, some new units would go a long way toward getting a lot of the homeless off the streets. Some of them have jobs, but they don't earn enough to pay rent and keep food on their tables."

"Charlotte has more than its share of those project places already," he said. "They're always building a new one, it seems. There's one about a mile on down Providence Road, in fact."

"There aren't nearly enough, Buck," Amie said patiently. "Anyway, I presented a plan that everybody seems interested in, only we have to buy this piece of property before anything official can be decided. When I tracked it down at the courthouse, I discovered that you own part of it. At least, the Camerons own it, and that includes you."

The minute she told him, she knew she'd picked the wrong time.

"So that's why you didn't back away from me."

His voice was cold as ice, and when she looked

and saw the scowl on his face, she froze. "What do you mean by that?" she asked.

"That scene in the bedroom. You were as anxious as I was to get there, weren't you? And I thought it was because you honest-to-God wanted me. *Me*. Not what I could do for you."

"You know better than that," Amie said, feeling her heart congeal.

"I don't know any such thing." He didn't look at her, only glared ahead. "How long have you had your eye on that property?"

Amie lifted her chin defiantly, her green eyes flashing.

"Answer my question. How long have you been trying to manipulate me?"

"*Manipulate* you?"

"Don't play the innocent with me, Amie." He lowered his voice to a threatening level. "You wouldn't be the first woman who wanted something from Buck Cameron. I guess I've been too damned blind to see it. Too . . ."

He pressed the accelerator, hating the thoughts that drove him blindly onward. How could he have let himself think she was different?

What was there about him that made *him* so damned different? That made women see him differently from the way his mother looked at his father, or the way he'd seen his brother's wife look at him?

Amie was like all the other women he'd known. If they didn't want sex, then it was something else. At least Amie was original. A piece of prime downtown property was something worth going after, even if she did want to give it away.

For a minute Amie wanted to strangle him. But then she realized how it must seem to him. She imagined he did get tired of having people hit on him, and this was not the first time she'd approached him for his help.

"I'm sorry, Buck," she said quietly, thankful her voice was steady. "I wanted that property before I even knew it belonged to the Camerons. When I went down to the courthouse and found the record of the deed, I was glad it belonged to someone I knew. It isn't being used, so I thought I'd ask you about it. That's all."

His hands clenched the steering wheel. He allowed a glance toward her. When he saw how distraught she appeared, he wished he could believe it was not an act.

"Forget the property, Buck," she said quietly. "Like you've told me before, I should approach things like this differently. I should have gone through the proper channels and not made it seem like a personal request."

"Sure," he said shortly. "We'll just forget it."

Amie tried to smile, but her lips felt frozen in a straight line.

Buck said nothing more, only stared ahead as they drove in silence. She'd meant to ask about Marsha, but decided they had enough between them right now without opening another hornet's nest.

NINE

The Cameron home was something of a surprise to Amie. From what she had been led to believe about the senior Camerons, she had expected a mansion with a conservative, formal facade. Though imposing, the two-story brick house with its big white columns seemed warm and inviting from the moment she saw it.

Large beds of azaleas were in bud in front of tall camellias that flanked the front. A carriage-house chandelier lit the wide, covered porch, and two containers, one on either side of the big double doors, were filled with an abundance of flowering bulbs.

Buck's mother answered the door when he rang the bell. "I insisted that I get the door when the bell rang," she said. "I knew it would be you." She held out her arms for Buck's hug.

She was close to Amie's height, but because she was in flat-heeled slippers, Buck had to bend down so she could kiss him on his cheek.

"I've been so anxious to see for myself that you're still in one piece, Buckley. I might have known you'd be late, as usual," she added, turning her warm smile on Amie.

They stepped inside and Amie saw immediately where part of Buck's good looks came from. His mother was a beautiful woman, younger than Amie had expected. Any gray in her brown hair was deceptively camouflaged by streaks of blond. It was straight like Buck's and she wore it in a short, fluffy style that flattered a high cheekboned, patrician face. Her gown was a muted abstract print in pale green and gold that emphasized the green in her bright hazel eyes.

"Mother," Buck said affectionately, "this is Amie Phillips. Amie, my mother, the one and only Caroline Cameron."

Though his words and actions were warm and friendly enough, when he looked at Amie his eyes seemed cold and impenetrable. So he hadn't forgiven her, after all.

Amie gave her attention to Caroline and felt the friendly scrutiny of her keen eyes. "I'm so glad Buckley brought you, Amie," she said simply. "Now, we'd best hurry. I insisted that everyone wait until you got here, Buckley, before we open the gifts."

Buck slipped his arm around his mother's shoulders and Amie walked beside them. She hoped she was successful at hiding her feelings. Buck was polite enough, but Amie was sensitive to the wall he'd put up between them. Had her carefully composed features revealed something of what she was feeling to Caroline Cameron? Was that the reason for the curious little smile on Caroline's face? Unwittingly, Amie lifted her chin.

Caroline led them past the formal living room to

a very warm and comfortable library where several people were standing around—the other family members, Amie assumed.

"Most everybody is out on the sun porch," Caroline said, nodding toward a door at the end of the room. "The buffet is set up out there."

"You go ahead, Mother," Buck said. "I see Wicket has Dad cornered and I'd like Amie to meet them first." He took Amie's elbow properly, formally.

Wicket was clearly much older than Buck, shorter by several inches, and though wide shoulders seemed to be a family trait, he was obviously not the athlete Buck was. His brown eyes crinkled at the corners when he smiled, and he made no pretense at hiding his wide grin when he saw Amie with Buck. It was J. Wicket, Sr. who did not smile.

"Amie, I'd like you to meet my dad," Buck said.

There was no mistaking the pride in Buck's voice, but there was something more—more, even than affection. Amie detected a real camaraderie between the two men.

"And this is my brother, Wicket."

"Well, well!" Wicket exclaimed. "Buck's always one for surprises, but he's outdone himself this time. What a pleasure it is to meet you, Amie."

She smiled and offered her hand, which Wicket took enthusiastically. When he released it, it occurred to her that she'd actually meant it for Buck's father, who was still standing quietly, looking at her in a most curious way. He cut his eyes to Buck, then returned his appraisal to her.

"How do you do, sir." She liked Buck's father immediately. She wasn't certain if it were instinctive because he reminded her so much of Buck, or if it was because she wanted him to like her.

His shock of unruly hair was snow white and his eyes were almost as blue as his son's, and every bit as penetrating. Amie knew she was being sized up, and it was important to her that she not fall short in his estimation. She also knew it was not simply because he was Buck's father. The senior Mr. Cameron, she was certain, was a man whose favor anyone would covet.

Even Buck noticed his father's long pause. "You'll have to forgive Dad," he said easily. "I think he's been caught off guard."

"Nonsense!" When he spoke, his voice had the same timbre as Buck's. "Nothing catches me off guard. I was trying to decide how to introduce myself. It's damned aggravating to have more than one Wicket about, Amie," he said. "I'd like it if you'd call me Josiah." Still, his expression was somber.

"My mother would think that scandalous," Amie said with an impish grin. "I was brought up to call only my peers by their given names."

"You're going to be in deep trouble if you try calling me *Mister* Cameron," he said, smiling for the first time.

And it was worth the wait, Amie thought, as she melted from the warmth of his accolade. "I wouldn't think of it," she replied. "It's always more fun doing things mama never taught me."

Josiah Wicket Cameron's laughter was even more pleasant than his smile. Amie noticed, though, that the mirth in his eyes suddenly gave way to something much softer. She turned to follow his gaze and saw Caroline approaching.

"Wicket, those boys of yours are too much for Barbara to handle all by herself," Caroline said to her older son. She slipped her arm through her husband's, then smiled at Buck. "Amie must be famished, Buckley. Why don't we open the gifts now, and then the two of you can have something to eat. And Amie hasn't met Barbara or the boys."

Amie was impressed by the way Caroline's three men hastened to take her suggestions. Wicket, with a smile and a nod to Amie, was off to give Barbara a hand. Josiah, Buck, and Amie immediately followed Caroline. Maybe there's something to be learned here, Amie thought with a smile.

The thought, however, was fleeting. It was clear to Amie that Caroline's husband and two sons were anxious to do her bidding because they loved her. This was no trick to be learned.

Amie glanced up at Buck. The only love between them came from her own heart, not his. She swallowed hard, refusing to let her mind dwell on it.

The sun room was a long L-shaped room with windows on three sides. A long buffet table against the one stuccoed wall was lit by tall candelabras, and ornate Mexican lanterns that hung from the high ceiling cast patterned shadows over the white tablecloths that covered at least a dozen small tables about the room.

"I thought you said this was to be a small family gathering," Amie whispered to Buck, wishing she had worn something a bit more festive.

"Everyone here is so close, I guess we think of them as family," Buck replied. "Wicket and I grew up with most of the younger ones." He laughed, but its ring wasn't true. "If you can still call us young, that is."

"Speech! Speech!" everyone began clamoring as they all gathered at one end of the room where a large table held an array of packages. "Yeah, Wick!

Tell us how you've managed to keep the smile on Carrie's face all these years!" someone shouted.

Amie, suddenly mortified, grasped Buck's arm with both hands. "I'm going to kill you for not reminding me," she whispered frantically. "I know it should have occurred to me, Buck, but I didn't bring a gift."

"That was for me to take care of, not you," he said.

His voice lacked its usual warmth, Amie thought, giving him a questioning look. Surely he didn't plan to give her the deep-freeze treatment all evening. She wasn't sure she could take that. Not when she'd given herself to him only a short time ago, with total abandonment and all her love.

"You don't know my parents, Amie," he said. "How would you be expected to know what to get them?"

"But . . ."

"But nothing. Don't worry about it."

"But . . ."

"I said not to worry about it. I took care of it." Weaving through the fifty-odd people in the room, Buck led Amie to where his mother and father were about to begin opening their gifts.

Buck's father said a few appropriate words, then kissed his wife while everyone clapped and a few of the men whistled.

When they began to open the gifts, all the overhead lights came on. For the first time, Amie could actually get a good look at all the guests. She was relieved to see most of the women were wearing dresses similar to hers. Only Caroline and a few others were in long gowns.

Standing beside Wicket was a lovely blonde Amie assumed was Barbara because she was holding the hand of a squirming little boy who appeared to be three or four years old. One that was maybe seven or eight was separated from his brother and in Wicket's tow, but he was reaching around his dad trying to poke the smaller boy in the back with his fingers.

Then Amie heard a familiar voice at her shoulder. For a minute she thought it was her imagination, but when the woman pushed past her, carrying a large gold-and-silver wastebasket, Amie froze.

"Here, Carrie," the woman said, setting the basket on the floor beside the table. "You can put the wrappings in this."

Amie may have been stunned, but her mind was recalling bits of conversations with facile accuracy. *He's out of your league, Amie. I'd hate to see you get hurt by somebody with his reputation. Their father deserves all the credit in that family—he and their grandfather. People like Buck always have a motive.* And then there was the lie she'd told Buck about not knowing where Amie was Friday afternoon.

While Amie stared at Marsha, she also remembered what Buck had said only a few minutes earlier. *Everyone here is so close, I guess we think of them as family.* And again, Marsha's taunt, "*He's out of your league, Amie.*"

"What is it?" Buck asked. "Your hand's cold as ice."

Amie couldn't look at Buck. Her eyes were riveted on Marsha. "I didn't know . . . Neither you nor Marsha ever mentioned that she and your family . . . You never told me that she was practically a family member. And this . . . this feud between the two of you. You've never explained that, and I'd think Marsha would've have said something to me by now."

She looked up at Buck and saw no indication that anything she'd said disturbed him.

"Marsha isn't the type to say much about her personal life to outsiders," he said.

Outsiders? Amie came unfrozen fast. Was that what he thought of her? An outsider? Then why in hell had he brought her here? She felt her hand grow rigid in his.

As if he were reading her mind—a knack that was presently offensive to Amie—he squeezed her hand. "Look here," he said in a gently commanding voice.

His tone was such an improvement, Amie looked up at him. He shook his head slowly, giving her a look that was at once a caress and a reprimand. "Anyone Marsha hasn't known since she was in diapers is an outsider to her," he whispered. "Surely that doesn't bother you?"

"No, but it is a surprise to see her here, especially when you've been so closemouthed about her."

"I didn't know she'd be here or I'd have mentioned it," he said. "Not that it should make any difference."

"Buckley!" Amie heard Caroline's voice. "Where in the world did you find this?" she asked, holding up an album she had unwrapped.

"You'll never believe it, Mother, but I found it in Peru. American beach music must not be as high on their list as it is on ours," he said, smiling.

"We've been trying to find these records for years, son," his father said, taking the album from Caroline.

"I was pretty sure they were the ones missing from your collection," Buck said.

"And you've already put it on a disc!" Caroline exclaimed, holding up the smaller item. "No," she said in a surprised tone. "This has Amie's name on it. Thank you, dear. That was very thoughtful of you."

Marsha chose that moment to look directly at Amie. Amie flushed, feeling guilty because the disc wasn't her own idea. "You shouldn't have done that, Buck," she said.

"Forget it. The folks know it was only a polite gesture," he said quietly.

Of course, Amie thought—a polite gesture. They wouldn't expect more than that from one of Buck's countless companions. She understood now why Caroline had looked at her so curiously. She could easily imagine the variety of women Buck had introduced to his mother, and the many others Caroline could only wonder about.

"Oh, Marsha, this is lovely," Caroline was saying. Amie watched as Buck's mother held up a small, original watercolor for everyone to admire. "You remembered," she said, hugging Marsha and kissing her on the cheek. Turning to her husband, she said, "I was admiring this only last week when Marsha and I were at the gallery's private showing of Bernard's work. Isn't it lovely?"

"Leave it to Marsha," Buck muttered beneath his breath, leaning close to Amie's ear so no one else would hear him. "She's probably spent a month's interest from her trust fund trying to impress Mother."

Amie made no comment. *He's not in your league, Amie.* Marsha's words came again to haunt her. It didn't help matters to know Marsha was right. Amie knew she could never have afforded such an expensive gift. She'd seen Bernard's work, though not at the private showing. That one little watercolor could have moved someone off the street and into a new apartment.

After another thirty minutes, all the gifts were opened and Buck and Amie were filling their plates with more food than Amie had seen in weeks. "We've pushed two tables together so there'll be room for the immediate family to sit together," Barbara said to them. "You don't have to put everything on your plate at once, Buck. You can always come back for seconds," she teased, tugging at his arm.

Amie grinned, looking down at her own plate. "I guess that goes for me, too," she said, deciding to forego the pâté she was about to sample. She looked up and saw Josiah standing beside her with a big smile on his face. His familiar expression was one she had seen on Buck's face, and she couldn't deny the potency of its charm. It was a pleasured smile, and Josiah's eyes sparkled with mischief.

"Go ahead," he encouraged. "There's plenty of room on that plate for one small cracker and a sample of Carrie's pâté." He reached around her and spread a wheat cracker with pâté. "Open," he said, popping the small cracker into her mouth.

"Why, Mr. Cameron. Shame on you for being such a bad influence," Amie said after she'd swallowed the treat.

"I thought we'd decided it's Josiah."

"I've noticed everyone else calls you Wick," she observed, spreading another cracker with the delicious oyster pâté.

"Everyone except you and Carrie," he replied, taking her arm.

Buck said nothing, simply concentrated on the plate he was still mounding high.

Wick, also without turning around, said, "Why don't you escort your sister-in-law back to the table,

Buck? You must have known that if you brought Amie, you'd have to sacrifice a little of her time."

"Where is Barbara?" Amie heard Buck ask as she and his father left him with Wicket.

"Let's take the long way back," Josiah suggested. "There's nothing at the table to drink except that damn fizzy champagne. We'll detour by the library, if it's all right with you, and I'll pour myself some fortification. I never could stand more than ten people in a room, and a little Scotch helps dull the noise."

"But it's your anniversary," Amie said. "Buck said that everyone here was like family."

"Humph! Not my family. The better part of them are nothing but ingrates." When they stepped into the library, Josiah slid the heavy doors together. "What's that smile about, Amie? I'm pretty sure you aren't the type to patronize an old man."

"I was thinking how much alike you and Buck are. And how do you know I wouldn't patronize you? I've been working very hard at learning how to play my politics, Josiah, and I imagine you're exactly the kind of person I'm supposed to practice on."

Josiah took a bottle of Scotch from a back corner of the liquor cabinet and poured some into a glass. "Four inches," he said, grinning when he turned his blue eyes on Amie. "I have to hide this bottle. Let 'em suspect you're getting old, Amie, and they start trying to measure out everything for you, including life. Trouble is, most people don't know how to live, even when they're young; so I do my own measuring." The devil danced in his indigo eyes. "To avoid a ruckus, I do as I please, but try to keep it to myself as much as possible."

"Typical politician, huh?"

After tossing half the Scotch down, Josiah chuckled. ''I see you're learning the tricks of the trade. I hope you aren't trying to practice on Buck,'' he said with a twinkle in his eyes. ''Something tells me you'd need more than a graduate degree to get away unscathed.''

Amie laughed but its sound was empty. ''You aren't telling me anything I don't already know,'' she said. ''I'm afraid my politics are quite different from your son's, and never the twain shall meet, as they say.''

Josiah raised his brow skeptically and she wished immediately that she hadn't said anything. He emptied his glass and put his arm affectionately around Amie's shoulders. ''He's no son of mine if he doesn't know how to compromise,'' he said, ''especially when he stands to gain so much.'' He gave her a wicked grin and a little squeeze. ''Or maybe I'm wrong,'' he said more seriously. ''Maybe my feeling that you and Buck seem so right for each other is no more than an old man's dream.''

''You're a worse flirt than Buck,'' Amie said teasingly, wishing she didn't like Buck's father so much. She couldn't forget Buck's accusing words, or the empty feeling that hearing them had given her. Most likely, she wouldn't be seeing much of Josiah Cameron.

''Buck's very much your son,'' Amie added, thinking how handsome Josiah Wicket was. ''Right down to the sexy blue eyes.''

''Just for that, you'll have to sit with me during dinner. And, of course, I expect to be an outrageous flirt.''

Josiah took his seat at the head of the two small tables that had been pushed together for the family.

Caroline was sitting at the other end with Barbara to her left and Buck to her right. Marsha was sitting next to Buck. Josiah put his plate down and set Amie's at the empty space to his right. This put Wicket next to her.

"I'm sitting next to Grandpa," little David piped up, sliding from his seat between his mother and father to come up from beneath the table on the other side. "That's your brother's place," Caroline said. "Move down one seat, David. That was supposed to be your place, anyway."

"Don't worry, Davy," Josiah said with a chuckle. "You'll still be able to see Amie from there."

"I don't want to sit next to Aunt Marsha!" Davy said. "I want Uncle Buck to sit where she is so he can tell me about the lions and the *ephalants*."

"Elephants," Marsha said sweetly.

"*Ephalants*. They're *ephalants*! And don't you tell me. Uncle Buck knows!" He began to scramble down from his chair.

"Here, I'll change places with Wicket," Buck said, pushing his chair back. "That'll put me and Amie across from Davy."

Caroline's hand closed around Buck's wrist. "Don't be ridiculous, Buckley. Josiah, do something with your grandson."

"It's all right, Mother," Buck said, looking down at her hand on his wrist. "I brought Amie, so I should sit beside her."

"We're fine down here, Buck," Amie said cheerfully, thinking she'd rather be next to a cobra. *I brought Amie, so I should sit beside her*. Another remark like that and she'd tell him what he could do with his obligation.

"Your father is giving me some badly needed lessons in politics,'' she said, ''and Davy wants to hear about my cats, don't you, Davy?''

''I don't want to sit beside Marsha!'' the little boy wailed, disappearing beneath the table and coming up between Amie's legs.

''Well, for goodness sakes, Buck!'' Marsha exclaimed when Buck lifted the wrist his mother clutched and gallantly kissed her hand before placing it on the table.

''Davy, march yourself right back to your seat,'' Wicket said sternly.

''No! I want to sit on Amie's lap.''

''So does your Grandpa,'' Buck said jovially, ''but Amie likes to clean her plate, just like you're going to do while we talk about *ephalants*,'' he said, to Davy's delight.

Picking up their plates as if they were used to musical chairs, Buck and Wicket exchanged places.

''Now, Davy,'' Amie said, picking up the boy, ''I'll take you to your seat and we'll all have our dinner.'' The boy seemed pleased with his victory, even though he still had Marsha to his left. Amie rather admired Barbara who, during the confusion, paid no attention to anything except her dinner.

''There,'' Buck said with amused satisfaction when Amie took her seat again. ''I can keep a better eye on you now, and there'll be no flirting between you and Dad.'' He winked at his father and added, ''Don't think I didn't see you close the doors when you took her into the library. And don't try to tell me it was only to snitch the Scotch.''

Josiah laughed and gave Amie a wink.

It was all very polite and Buck continued to show her the deference he would any woman he'd brought to his family's home. But the devil was gone from his blue eyes, and Amie knew that meant the warmth from his heart was gone, too. By the end of the evening, she was exhausted from biting her tongue and from holding back the tears.

"It was very nice having you with us tonight, Amie," Caroline Cameron said at the door when Amie and Buck were leaving.

Amie didn't doubt her sincerity, but she didn't miss the question in her eyes when Josiah hugged her and said, "I'll give you another lesson in politics the next time you're here, Amie. And make that soon, son," he said to Buck, laying his hand on his shoulder. The warmth of Josiah's hug was lost, though, when Amie looked up and saw Buck's eyes. Her reflection was not in them.

In the quietness of the car, Amie reflected on the evening. It would have been impossible to miss the closeness that existed between Caroline and Marsha. Caroline had even made a place at the family table for her. Not once had Marsha brought up the fact that she and Amie worked together, and nothing personal passed between them during the dinner conversation. Amie was at a loss to understand what she now referred to in her mind as "The Marsha Thing." But she intended to clear that up right now.

Breaking the silence, she asked, "You said you and Marsha have known each other since you were both in diapers?"

"I didn't mean that literally," he said, keeping his eyes on the road ahead. "Marsha's mother was one of my mother's best friends, and Charles, Marsha's husband, was Wicket's fraternity brother. Mother and Kathleen were determined to marry Marsha off to one of us, so Wick and I ganged up on Charles and managed to get the two of them together."

When he laughed, Amie's breath caught. He sounded like the Buck she loved. "I don't believe that for a minute," she chided. "I'll bet Marsha could have had her pick of the three, and you and Wick like to think you were the ones who did the rejecting." Amie could not discount the fact that Marsha was single again, and Buck was very much a bachelor. "What, exactly, happened to Charles?" she asked.

"He was always trying to get me to take him and Marsha with me to Kenya," Buck said. "I couldn't think of a worse idea, and I kept refusing. Charles thought hunting deer qualified him to go after big game.

"I did everything I could to dissuade him. I tried to tell him that he had neither the temperament nor the talent for something like that, let alone the constitution. But I think Marsha put him up to it in the first place because it sounded glamorous to her . . . exciting, she kept saying, as if she knew all about excitement and where to find it.

"Finally, Mother joined in the persuasion, so I thought, what the hell, I'll take them and get them all off my back. I made it clear that once we were there, they could join one of the safaris, but that I wanted no part of it.

"They had to go outside the Mara to hunt, and they weren't supposed to be back for ten days. I left on my own, planning to meet them when their group was due back. So it took a couple of days for the news to catch up to me. Charles was killed in an elephant stampede—he and two others."

"Oh, Buck, how awful!" She saw Buck's jaw tighten. "And Marsha blamed you."

"Ummm. Well, shortly after the funeral Marsha's

mother had a stroke and didn't respond after being in intensive care for almost a month. After her death, Mother sort of adopted Marsha."

She knew it was resentment she detected in his voice, and little wonder. With Marsha blaming him, and so unjustly, she could imagine what it must be like to have to be around her so much. Now she understood why Marsha had said so many ugly things about Buck, and why she'd lied about Amie's whereabouts Friday afternoon. She understood, but she couldn't excuse Marsha.

They were silent for awhile, then Buck glanced toward her. "You and Dad seemed to hit it off tonight," he said.

"I like him a lot. I like your mother, too, but I had the feeling she preferred to reserve her opinion of me. Being a mother, I guess she doesn't see the women you take there the same way your father does."

As if he were doing nothing more than giving her a weather report, he said, "You're the first woman I've wanted to take there. That's why Mother was so polite to you all evening. Usually, she talks as much as you do, but she doesn't quite know how to take you yet."

Silently, she reminded herself that it didn't mean a thing. He'd taken her simply to see his family's reaction. She knew Buck liked to surprise people, and she was certain his family was used to it by now.

Now Amie understood what Buck either refused to see, or preferred to ignore. It was natural that Caroline should hope for Buck and Marsha to become a couple especially when Marsha was almost like a daughter to her already.

Buck and Marsha. No, that would never work, Amie thought, laying her head on Buck's shoulder only to feel him flinch. So, he really meant it when he accused her of using him. Nothing had changed. Quickly, she moved away from him.

"I suppose you're tired?" he asked shortly.

"Not really," she replied, trying hard to keep the quiver from her voice. Looking out the window, she had never felt so lonely. The need to touch him, to feel his arms around her, to be close to him in every way possible was overpowering.

"If you don't mind, I think I'll drop you by your place," he said. "I guess driving in the race and then rushing back to Charlotte took more out of me than I realized."

"Of course, I don't mind," Amie said, still not looking at him. "I'm surprised you made it through the evening."

When he pulled up in front of her house she almost fell out the door, she opened it so quickly. "I'll see myself in, Buck. I really appreciate you letting me share the evening with you and your family. It was a lovely dinner."

"I'll wait here until I know you're safely inside," he said.

"That's not necessary," replied Amie, then turned and hurried to her door. He did wait, she noticed, but she didn't look back, not even after she'd closed the door. With the back of her hand, she wiped the tears from her cheeks and went to the hall closet to find a blanket. There was no way she could sleep in her bed tonight. Not when it was still rumpled from their making love.

TEN

During the next week and a half, Amie ran the emotional gamut. At work, she continued the seemingly never-ending struggle to find aid for the homeless. There, she was quietly shunned by Marsha, who had barely spoken to her since the night they'd had dinner with the Camerons. Amie knew she should say something to Marsha, try to clear the air. But for the present, she decided it was just as well that Marsha was keeping to herself for the most part.

Away from work, she went through the motions of her necessary chores. She went to the grocery store to get cat food, to the dry cleaners, and to the car wash. Her apartment sparkled from being cleaned so much, and her muscles ached from long bouts with the weights at the health club. At home, she often found herself staring out her kitchen window.

She tried to be angry with Buck. Actually, she succeeded quite well for the first day or so. It was the only way she could deal with her hurt. She had to admit, though, that while she felt Buck's reaction was exaggerated, his anger was understandable. It had never occurred to her that he might feel she was trying to use him. And in his place, she might feel the same way.

But enough was enough. Damn it, if he had any real feeling for her, he'd have called by now.

At the end of the first week, Amie called Whitney Crawford. "I'm really sorry," she told him, "but I didn't do very well with Buck Cameron." *No, not very well at all.* "I don't think anyone will be able to persuade him to sell that downtown property. I'll try to come up with an alternative, Mr. Crawford."

And she did try. During her lunch hours she drove around the city looking for a satisfactory location for a housing project. There simply was none. The only other area that offered the convenience of easily accessible shopping and medical care had already been earmarked by the city for a proposed football stadium. To expect people to give up their toys, she knew, was out of the question.

Finally, as the days dragged by and Wednesday of the second week stared bleakly through her kitchen window, she had to face the reality that Buck was not going to call her.

She'd been warned, hadn't she? Not only by Tom and Millie, but by Marsha, as well. But she'd thought she was way ahead of them. She'd had a plan.

Her short laughter sounded hollow, much like the decision she'd made to turn the tables on Buck. She would be the hunter, not the hunted. Now she had no choice but to face the truth. She had failed.

Her colossal mistake was falling in love with Buck. She never meant for that to happen. And her second mistake was losing her perspective. For Buck, it was only a game. She knew that from the start, but somewhere along the way she lost sight of this important fact. She let her heart take the lead and made herself the loser. As a hunter, she denied herself the slightest chance.

Buck stalked her, then shot her down. And he hadn't even waited around to collect his trophies: her heart, her soul, her love. They meant so little to him, he'd grabbed at the first viable straw he could use as an excuse and walked away from her. Well, it was no more than she deserved. She shouldn't have made herself such an easy target.

Glancing at the clock, she knew she'd have to hurry or be late for work. On the way to her bedroom to collect her purse and her briefcase, her steps became more determined. Taking the phone directory from her bedside table, she looked up the number for Cameron, Inc.

"Yes?" Kristen Wells asked when she answered her phone.

Having gone through the receptionist, Amie assumed this would be Buck's secretary. She repeated her request to speak with him.

"Phillips. Amie Phillips. Of course," Kristen said. She was certain it was the do-gooder. She smiled, knowing she'd have to make the best of this opportunity. "Mr. Cameron's in New York for a board meeting," Kristen said. "Is there any message?"

"No. No, there's no message," Amie replied.

Not good, thought Kristen. "Ms. Phillips?"

"Yes?"

Did she dare? Kristen wondered, knowing she'd have the devil to pay if it backfired. "I thought I recognized your name, and it's no wonder. It's scribbled right here on my notepad. Mr. Cameron asked me to tell you he's working on that problem of yours, and he'll be back in Charlotte by the end of the week."

"That *problem* of mine?"

"He didn't explain himself. I assumed you'd understand."

"I see," said Amie, not seeing at all. "Well, thank you, Ms. . . ."

"Wells. Kristen Wells. I'm Mr. Cameron's secretary."

Amie was surprised when she walked into her office that morning and saw Marsha waiting for her. Was she there to wield the proverbial axe? "Good morning," Amie said.

"We can't go on like this," Marsha began abruptly.

"I know, Marsha." Amie dropped into the chair behind her desk. "Things aren't working out with us, are they?"

"Of course, they are," Marsha said with determination. "We work well together. It's only that . . ." She glanced down at her hands, then back at Amie. "I owe you an apology. It really upsets me that I've let something personal interfere with our professional relationship."

"This isn't necessary," Amie insisted. "I've been thinking about it all week, Marsha, and it isn't just this . . . this grudge you hold against Buck that's gotten in our way. I cause problems by getting too involved with my work, I know that. I lose my objectivity and that's no good in a job like ours. The worst of it is, I don't see any prospects of changing. I've tried, and I don't seem to get anywhere with it.

And I'm always coming up with these great plans that I can't make work."

"You do expect miracles sometimes, but you pull one off every now and then. I still can't believe you talked the Humane Society into letting that family of five move into the grounds cottage in back of their facility. And they hired the father. What was it they said he'd be? A sanitation engineer? Come on, Amie. The only thing that guy knows about engineering is how to hook up the plumbing to make three children."

Despite Marsha's laughter, Amie remained solemn. "It was the only job title on their list that they'd been given funds for," Amie said. "And he will be taking care of sanitation."

"Yeah. Hosing down the animal quarters."

"Anyway, you'd have come up with something for them if I hadn't been here," Amie said. "And without getting yourself in even deeper by promising to help them furnish the cottage."

"You've gotten me sidetracked," Marsha said. "What I really wanted to talk to you about is Buck."

Amie cringed. "So what about him?"

"It goes back to when my husband was killed."

"Buck told me about the accident," she said. "You don't have to go into all that."

"He told you about our being in Africa together?"

Amie didn't want to talk about Buck, and especially not with Marsha. "Before you go any further, I should tell you that Buck and I won't be seeing each other anymore," she said. "We don't see eye to eye on many things, and it's hard to build a relationship with so little in common. You were right about one thing," she said with a sigh. "Buck and I aren't in the same league."

Marsha frowned. "I hope you didn't misunderstand when I said that. You're such a straight arrow, Amie, or at least that's the impression you always give me. I couldn't imagine your having anything to do with Buck, that's all. He has such a reputation with the women. He's tossed over at least a dozen I know of, and I've even heard rumors that he supports that woman in Peru."

That woman in Peru? "What Buck does or doesn't do is none of my concern," Amie said, "but thanks for trying to clear the air."

Marsha appeared to be relieved. "Friends?" she asked with an appealing smile.

"Of course," Amie replied, hoping her composure wouldn't crumble. She remembered asking Buck about his friends in Peru. She also remembered his evading her question.

"Now that we're friends again," she said with a forced smile, "will you please help me think of something to do about the young couple who were in here yesterday who are expecting a baby? Do you think maybe we can find a place for them to stay until the guy can get a job?"

"I'll check all my records. If I find a possibility, I'll let you know."

When Amie's phone rang she was relieved to end her conversation with Marsha. Millie was on the other end of the phone, determined to talk her into going with her to the re-opening of Spirit Square, the city's arts center. Amie didn't feel like going to an opening. She didn't feel like doing anything now that she knew the real reason behind Buck's disappearing act. He was already committed. *To that woman in Peru.*

And he'd had the nerve to accuse Amie of using

him. Buck Cameron was lowdown and dirty. And the hole in Amie Phillips' head was big enough to accomodate a stampede of wild *ephalants*.

"Are you still there, Amie?" Millie wanted to know. "You can forget it if you're trying to dream up a reason not to go with me. Unless Buck called, of course."

"You can't seem to get it through your head that Buck won't be calling me," Amie said. "How many times do I have to tell you that?"

"Snippy, aren't you?" Millie said accusingly. "It seems to me you care more about Buck than you're willing to admit."

"You sure can be pesky, can't you? For your information, I couldn't care less about Buck Cameron."

"Amie, you do care, don't you? Oh, honey. I'm really sorry."

"Will you stop it?" Amie's voice rose an octave before she caught herself. "You're imagining something that isn't there."

"I've known you most of our lives," Millie said, "so don't tell me what I know and what I don't."

"Well, there's one thing you don't know," Amie said. "He has someone special in Peru. From what I understand, someone he takes care of. You know what that means."

"I don't believe that," Millie said adamantly. "When Tom and I warned you about Buck, we didn't say he was a cad, did we? Only that he's wild and woolly. There's a difference, you know."

"I got this firsthand," Amie said, "and if it's all the same to you, I've had enough talk about Buck Cameron today."

"Okay," Millie said breezily. "Suits me. Only I'll see you Friday night, no ifs, ands, or buts."

* * *

"So, how's your week been since Wednesday?" Millie asked Friday evening as she adjusted the veil on the jaunty little black hat she wore atop her short auburn curls.

"It was okay," Amie said, looking around her living room for her purse.

"Well, you wouldn't know it to look at you." Millie eyed her from head to toe. "You look like hell. And what are you doing? Can't you ever keep up with that purse of yours? Now, let's do something about the way you look."

"Have I ever told you that you can be a real bitch when you try?" Amie said. "I'm not in the mood for this tonight."

Nonplussed, Millie sauntered past Amie. "That's why I'm such a good friend," she said to her glaring best friend. "I tell it like it is. And right now, you're going to change from that dowdy work suit into something that tells who the real Amie is. Then maybe you can find your smile. I won't have you moping around any longer feeling sorry for yourself. It's bad for my morale."

"I'm not doing that," Amie said, unable to suppress the smile Millie could always coax from her.

"Oh, yes, you are. And I'll not have it. I don't care who says Buck Cameron has a woman in Peru, I don't believe it. And you shouldn't, either, unless he tells you himself. So, stop moping and get a move on."

Amie had to laugh. She was the last person to mope and Millie knew it. "Just because I was hurt doesn't mean I was moping," she said.

"Yeah, well, we aren't dealing with a Joe Cannon here. You didn't love Joe, but it's pretty obvious that you do love Buck Cameron. So you're going to have to do something about it."

"You're taking a lot for granted," said Amie. "And I thought I loved Joe, so it didn't make it any easier when I had to admit that I'd been in a loveless relationship."

"So, when the real thing did come along, you had to go blow it."

"Damn it, Millie. It was as much his fault as it was mine. Maybe more his fault. He was looking for an excuse to walk away with no strings attached, and I helped him manufacture one. That's all."

"Ummm. Maybe," Millie said with a gleam in her eyes. "Now, hurry and change."

Amie glanced down at herself, noting the conservative navy suit she was wearing. "I don't look very festive, do I?" she asked with a chuckle.

"That's perfect for a wake," Millie agreed with a toss of her head. "This shindig is special. It cost big bucks to re-do the center, so everybody'll be showing off tonight."

"Then give me a minute," Amie said, noting the smart black velvet suit Millie was wearing.

When she appeared a few minutes later, Millie grinned. "Smashing, kiddo," she exclaimed, giving herself credit for the transformation.

Amie laughed, turning slowly for her best friend to admire her champagne silk skimmer. Although its lines were straight and simply cut on the diagonal, it did little to hide the curves beneath the fabric. With it she was wearing new elbow-length kid gloves—white, to match her pumps, which sported outrageously big rhinestone buckles. From her ears dangled huge sparkly earrings which came almost to the level of her chin.

"So where's Tom tonight?" Amie asked on the way out to the car.

"The ethics board is meeting at the hospital," Millie replied. "He promised to drop by Spirit Square if they let out soon enough."

"See?" Millie said excitedly when they finally found a parking space and exited the car. "Everyone turned out for this exhibition. The photographer's one of our own. He's lending his work for our opening before it's sent to New York."

"Who is he?" Amie asked.

"You'll get to see him," replied Millie. "He's supposed to be here tonight." Her face brightened. "I think you'll get a kick out of this."

Amie was certain they'd be squashed by the throngs inside. "The people here don't skimp when it comes to giving their support to civic affairs, do they?" Then she remembered how hard it often was to get help for Crisis House. "I wish they were as enthusiastic about the homeless as they seem to be about everything else," she added on a lower key.

They ambled past some interesting pieces of metal sculpture that were mounted on the walls of the hallway leading into the main gallery. "I'm glad you could come with me," Millie said. "Openings are always special. This one lends quite a bit of prestige to the city. I understand it'll be featured in all the largest cities before going on tour in Europe sometime next year."

Amie looked up from the large piece of sculpture she'd stopped to admire. "Didn't you say the photography's the work of one of our locals?"

"Uh-huh. But don't let the fact that he's home grown dim your appreciation of his work. He's considered by many to be one of the world's finest natural history photographers. I'm surprised you don't already know that." Looking at Amie slyly, she asked, "Or do you? Could it be that you've chosen to ignore that fact?"

"I don't know why," Amie said. "You know I'm not a photography buff."

"But this is something special. You'll see."

Amie looked around and was reminded of the first time she saw Buck at the Heart Ball. Sprinkled among those who wore their finest were the free spirits who were happy in their jeans and sneakers. For a moment her smile faded. Would she ever go anywhere again without being reminded of Buck?

Millie directed Amie to the buffet table where a fountain of champagne centered a lavish array of hors d'oeuvres. A lovely middle-aged woman put her hand on Millie's arm. "I'm so glad you could make it," the woman said, letting her gaze wander to Amie.

"I wouldn't have missed it for the world," Millie said with a big, conspiratorial smile. "Kristen, I'd like you to meet my very best friend, Amie Phillips. Amie, this is Kristen Wells."

Kristen Wells. "You're . . ."

"Yes. We spoke on the phone," Kristen said, taking Amie's hand. "I'm so happy to meet you, Amie. Did you just arrive?"

"We haven't had time to . . . *see* anything," said Millie.

"Oh, goodness. Then don't let me keep you," Kristen said, giving Millie a meaningful look. "Perhaps I'll see you both later."

"Amie!" came another voice as Kristen turned into the crowd. "How nice to see you here."

Amie turned toward the soft voice at her shoulder. "Caroline," she said self-consciously. "What a nice surprise." Feeling very awkward, Amie was almost happy to see Marsha with Caroline. She could think of nothing to say to Buck's mother, not even idle chatter.

Bejewelled in a bright silk print, Marsha was standing close beside Caroline. "Is Tom on call tonight, Millie?"

"He had a meeting with the ethics committee," Millie replied. "Hopefully, he'll join us later." Turning to Caroline, Millie said, "We're just now getting here, Mrs. Cameron. I hope you'll forgive me for dragging Amie away so we can admire the exhibit." Taking Amie's arm, Millie steered her away and through the crowd. "I hope we didn't appear rude," she said to Amie. "I didn't think you'd want to tarry there. Anyway, you haven't seen the photographs yet."

"I owe you one," Amie said, relieved that she didn't have to make small talk with Caroline and Marsha. Meeting Buck's secretary was enough. And she couldn't have been wrong about the looks that passed between Kristen and Millie. She supposed it was inevitable that Kristen should know she'd been out with Buck. Was that what she was verifying with Millie? That this was Amie Phillips, her boss's latest conquest?

"I don't know why, but seeing Kristen and then Caroline was almost like running into Buck," Amie said.

Millie nodded. "I think that's a normal reaction, honey. Here," she said, guiding Amie into the main gallery.

"It's really wonderful so many people turned out

for this,'' Amie said, overwhelmed by the size of the crowd. She was even more stunned when she saw the giant photographs that dominated the gallery. ''They're breathtaking,'' she said, staring with wide eyes at the color photographs that captured, with an evocative sensitivity, a spectacle of wildlife that left her in awe.

''He's better than Claus Kimmer,'' Amie heard someone behind her say. ''I've never seen better shots than these.''

''I understand they're good friends,'' another voice commented.

''I wonder if Becker came for the opening.''

''I thought I saw them together when we first came in,'' the first voice said.

''We could follow the strobes,'' the second suggested with a chuckle. ''The media's having a field day with this.''

Better shots than these. Shots . . . shots . . . Amie pushed through the crowd to get closer to a particular photograph of thousands of strange-looking animals trying to cross a wide river. ''Wildebeest,'' she murmured. ''These are the gnu Buck told me about . . . that he photographed in Africa.''

''They're what?'' Millie asked.

''Wildebeest. Gnu is the plural. Buck has this very same photograph at his house, only . . .'' Only he said *he* took the photograph. *I spent almost a week waiting to get this scene.*

''Amie, I see Tom,'' Millie said hastily. ''I'd better get him before he loses himself in this crowd.'' Then she spun on her heels, clutching Amie's arm. ''I know you'll thank me for bringing you,'' she said quickly. ''Maybe not tonight, but you *will* thank me.''

Amie stared at Millie's back with bewilderment. Now what on earth did she mean by that? she wondered, then turned to move to the next photograph. It was the pair of mating lions. Her heart beat faster and faster. She took a long, gasping breath.

"If that's your favorite, you can have the original."

She stared at the heavy signature scrawled on the photograph at the same time she heard his voice.

Buck Cameron.

She hadn't seen him in more than two weeks. Her heart raced. Slowly, she turned around.

How handsome he was in his unconventional attire. Anyone might have expected the guest of honor—the artist who was the center of all this commotion—to be dressed to the nines. Instead, here was Buck in his jeans and soft leather boots. But this, she knew, was his own turf. It would be blasphemy if he looked any different.

The diagonally buttoned suede shirt gave him an offbeat, rakish look, emphasizing the broad shoulders she knew inch by inch. Its smoky-blue color softened the brilliance of the eyes that were making promises she didn't want to think about. Damn him. He had no right. Yet her fingers ached to run through the thick brown hair at the nape of his neck, to curve around that strong neck . . .

"You look wonderful," he said, letting his gaze drift over the soft curves that were glorified by the clinging silk fabric of her dress. His eyes lingered at certain strategic points before they stopped to rest on the curve of her mouth, making her too conscious of his familiarity with her body, which he had previously, and so expertly, mapped.

"You never told me you were a celebrity," she said with as much composure as she could manage.

His eyes met hers and he gave her a small, reproving smile. Amie sensed he knew she was trying to distance herself from him.

"Celebrity? I like to think my work is worth celebrating, but me? You know better than that, darlin'."

She wanted to tell him not to call her that, but she couldn't because then she might be called on to explain why, and she couldn't tell him that its sound made her heart break in two.

"I'm glad you came," he said softly. "It means a lot to me . . . a lot." He reached to finger a lock of her hair and the back of his hand brushed her cheek. She shuddered.

"Kristen said you called. I behaved badly the other night, darlin', and I'm sorry. Your call made me happy." He grinned and her insides turned to liquid Jell-O. "I called you as soon as I got in today, but you'd already left. I'd hoped you'd come with me tonight." His gaze held her, refusing to let her look away.

Damn him. Did he think he could leave her the way he did that night and pick her up again as if nothing had happened? Had it never occurred to him that Marsha would tell her about the woman in Peru? And to accuse her of trying to use him. Who did he think was using whom?

Conscious of the stares of people around them, she said, "It's better that I came with Millie."

The sudden bleakness in his eyes made her stifle the cry that nearly choked her. Maybe she'd misjudged him. Could Marsha be wrong about the other woman? She had said it was *rumored*.

Stop it, she told herself, knowing she was on the verge of making a bigger fool of herself. Marsha would never have mentioned something like that if she hadn't been sure of her facts. Undoubtedly, Caroline had told her.

Unwittingly, Amie raised her hand to touch his arm, but it only floundered in midair as a tall man with heavy brows sheltering warm brown eyes stepped between them.

"Why is it you always corner the most beautiful woman in the room before I even get to meet her?" he asked with a smile big enough to brighten the whole gallery.

"Amie Phillips, this is Claus Kimmer," Buck said. "Claus introduced me to the wildlife of East Africa."

"And he's been trying to outdo me ever since," Claus said with obvious admiration. "I have to admit that his work is impressive," he added. Giving Amie a look of appraisal as he put his arm around Buck's shoulder, he said with a wink, "Mind you, it's not because he's a better photographer, but because of that special rapport he's developed with wild things."

Amie had no control over the smile that lit her face.

"They know he loves 'em, I guess," Claus said. "Most of the hunters only tolerate him, he gives them so much hassle about their sport."

Buck's voice was passionate when he spoke. "If they have to kill something, they should hunt each other. Then they might learn the terror of being shot at . . . maybe, even, what it's like to die."

Amie was in such a state of shock she didn't fully appreciate Claus's joke when he nodded toward the photograph of the lion and lioness. "I've never understood how he happens to shoot so many scenes of copulation. It must make a significant statement, eh, old buddy?'' Flashing his smile, he gave Buck an affectionate pat on the back.

How, Amie wondered, could she ever have made such a mistake? How did she manage to jump to the conclusion that Buck hunted these animals for the kill, especially after seeing the photographs in his home? From the very beginning she should have realized that a gun is not the only thing that *shoots*.

''Don't mind him, Amie,'' Buck said. ''Claus is happily married. That's why his shots lack the elements of erotica.''

And why yours don't, Amie thought. She hadn't missed Claus's allusion to Buck's prowess with women.

How could she still want him? Even now, knowing how little she must mean to him despite the charm he poured over her, she was still shaken by desire.

''I hate to interrupt this,'' Claus said, ''but I promised your local TV station that the two of us would give them an interview before I have to leave. And since the limousine's waiting to take me to the airport, it looks like this is it, old buddy.''

''You know how I hate interviews,'' Buck complained.

''A favor, then? Come on, Buck.'' He tugged at Buck's arm, directing his next words to Amie. ''I always interfere when he's trying to make a conquest, Amie, and he never forgives me. Right, old buddy?'' He turned toward Buck just in time to take the full blast of the daggers Buck's eyes shot him. Claus laughed. ''I promise I'll make it up to you.''

''Yeah, like you always do,'' Buck said with a blend of irritation and affection.

''Hey!'' Claus exclaimed. ''Have you forgotten the time in Peru . . .'' He stopped short when he caught the dark expression that veiled Buck's eyes. "Just this once," he said quickly. "Honest, Buck, I need the publicity for my new book."

Buck looked at Amie and shrugged. "Will you wait here for a few minutes?" he asked.

"Sure she will," Claus answered for her. "When have you ever had a woman run out on you?"

Buck appeared uncomfortable. Amie smiled, hoping he found Claus's remarks as unnerving as she did. Maybe he realized a couple of life's verities—there's a first time for everything, and not every woman was ready to put her life on hold for him.

"Look," Buck said, touching her arm. "Why don't you find Mother and say hello to her? This won't take more than five minutes, at the most."

"I have to go, Buck." She said it quickly while Claus's presence helped bolster her courage. "It was nice to meet you," she said to Claus, avoiding Buck's compelling eyes.

Claus put his hand on Buck's shoulder and seemed genuinely surprised when Buck shrugged it away.

"Amie?" Buck said with a deep groan.

There was no mistaking the trace of angry impatience in his voice. She wasn't certain whether it was meant for her benefit, or Claus's. "Go with Claus," she said. "I'll wait."

She had never lied to Buck, certainly not the way she suspected he'd lied to her. And she didn't intend this to be an untruth. She would wait—alone. Most likely forever, though Buck wouldn't know. But not here, not tonight. She knew with the same certainty she knew the sun would rise tomorrow that if she saw him again tonight she wouldn't have the strength or the desire to say no if he asked her to leave with him. And her instincts told her that was exactly what he had in mind. Buck didn't like to lose at anything. Not even, she imagined, at the game some called love.

As Buck and Claus disappeared through the crowd, she looked around for Millie and Tom. They were nowhere to be seen. In a way she was glad. She knew Millie's bringing her to the opening was calculated. She had left Amie alone when she saw Buck coming toward them, and she would want to know what had happened between them. Amie didn't feel like making explanations tonight. She found a phone and called a taxi.

No one was in the long hall that led to the front lobby. The echo of Amie's footsteps on the marble floor taunted her, chasing her from behind, then up the walls and across the ceiling, running faster than her own feet. She escaped them only when she reached the black-and-white tile lobby and stood watching through the swinging glass doors for the taxi to arrive. Her feet stilled, but her heart did not.

ELEVEN

"What are you doing? Running out on me?"

Amie clutched the steel bar on the door behind her as she whirled toward him. Her eyes found the exit sign down the hallway.

"Forget it. You're leaving with me." His strong fingers circled her wrist. "Now."

"You're crazy!" She tightened her grip on the bar. "You can't leave. You're the guest of honor. The media has this place saturated."

"To hell with the media." His expression was dark, determined. "Let's go."

She remembered the night at the Heart Ball when he'd asked her to leave with him. This time was different; he was not asking. She could go or risk an argument, and the heat in his eyes left no doubt as to who would win. She was not surprised when he seemed to read her mind.

"I should've dragged you away from that Heart Ball the first time I saw you. It would have saved a helluva lot of time." Holding on to her wrist, he pushed against the swinging doors.

"Saved time for what?" The harshness of her own voice surprised her. "I knew you were crazy the minute I laid eyes on you. I didn't need time to discover that."

Buck hurried her along beside him toward his car. "I'm damned tired of hearing how crazy you think I am," he said, holding her while he unlocked the car door. He pulled her directly in front of him, and his voice was softer when he spoke again. "I know I shouldn't have taken you home and left you the way I did after the dinner with my folks. I wanted to explain how I felt, but I didn't know how. Hell, maybe I didn't want to then. I admit I'm stubborn, always have been, but that doesn't mean I can't work on it. I'm sorry, Amie. So damned sorry. Doesn't that mean anything?"

"Only that you're *sorry*," she said, emphasizing the last word.

He laughed. Threw his head back and laughed. He didn't sound like a guilty man. Again, she wondered if Marsha could be wrong. She knew she'd have to ask him, but not right now. For the moment, the fire was already too hot.

"Maybe she was right," Buck said.

"What?"

"Kris. She said I was wrong about you."

"Kris?" She looked heavenward. The man had women stashed everywhere. Then she remembered. Kristen Wells.

"My secretary," he explained. "I referred to you once as a do-gooder. Later, she pointed out that I was wrong to label you."

"That was nice of her," Amie said, wondering

why Kristen would argue in her favor. "I called your office a day or so ago and she told me you'd be back today. I never expected to see you here." She wondered if she'd have come, knowing he'd be here. Her eyes squeezed shut with the knowledge that nothing could have kept her away. And she'd accused *him* of being crazy. "Kristen also told me you were working on my problem. What, exactly, is that supposed to mean?"

"Kristen told you that?" He looked surprised. "Well, I haven't solved it yet, and I'm not about to tell you until I do."

"Then why . . ." She closed her mouth. Hadn't she learned by now that if he didn't want to tell her something, she'd never get a straight answer to any question she asked about it? Again, she tried to wrench free of his grasp.

"It's my own problem I need to work on right now," Buck said, letting go of her wrist only to take her by the shoulders.

"You're impossible," she murmured as he drew her roughly into his arms.

"Not where you're concerned." He tightened his grip, leaned her against the side of the car and closed in on her. His warm, wine-scented breath was intoxicating. The thin silk of her dress left little to the imagination when he pressed against her. "See what I mean?"

The pure sensuality in his voice had an unnerving effect that, coupled with his obvious desire, made Amie forget all the misery he'd caused her. She no longer wanted to escape him. She wanted him. Urgently. Desperately. "Damn you," she said, hating the sob that caught in her voice.

He gave her a sudden, weary smile, and she saw

how physically tired he was. She imagined that chairing a board meeting and then having to come to an opening as guest of honor on his first night back in town had taken their toll.

He laid his cheek against hers. ‘‘Do you have any idea how much I've missed you?’’ he asked, nuzzling her face.

‘‘If you missed me so much, why didn't you call?’’

His lips brushed her cheek. ‘‘I should have, I guess. I wanted to look you in the eyes when I tried to explain why I behaved like such a fool.’’ He moved his head so she could see his face. ‘‘Hell, honey. I've never cared when women used me before. I expected them to. It was sort of a mutual understanding, you know? Give and take.’’

‘‘Then you still believe that's what I was trying to do.’’

‘‘No. No, that's not what I believe.’’ His voice was strained and low, and his eyes as unreadable as his thoughts. ‘‘I should have known better, should never have believed for a minute that you could ever use anyone. Amie, I'm truly sorry.’’

He was so close she could see the flutter of his lashes.

‘‘Please say you forgive me.’’

His voice was as soft as the warm, sweet scent of May that flirted with the cool breeze ruffling Amie's hair. A spiral of longing parted her lips for the kiss that hovered on Buck's mouth. But he didn't kiss her.

‘‘I've waited too long for this to make love to you in a parking lot,’’ he said. ‘‘We can be home in less than thirty minutes.’’

* * *

They sped through the city streets in silence. Once, when they stopped for a red light, Amie felt Buck's eyes burn through her. She didn't dare look toward him for fear he'd see her quiet desperation. Desperation born from knowing she was helplessly in love. Desperation compounded by the knowledge that sooner or later she'd be alone again. *Again*.

How long would it last this time, she wondered. One night? Two? And then what? When he began to feel restless would he fly off to Africa, or more likely to Peru, and tell her he had to go on a business trip? Next time, it would be even worse. Could she survive a next time?

The worst part was knowing she'd already made up her mind. How could she refuse him when every fiber of her body strained for him? Already there was a dampness between her thighs. Her breasts ached. She throbbed. All over.

They reached the outskirts of the city. Leaving the street lights behind, they plunged into a pitch-black darkness except for the headlights of the car that shot ahead of them. "Have you forgiven me yet?" Buck asked finally.

The gentleness of his voice prodded her, but she kept her face turned away. "It's over and done. Let's try to forget it."

"You can't forget without forgiving, Amie."

"What about you, Buck? The words sound good, but do you know in your heart that I could never use you?"

"Not even my body?" He cocked a brow and grinned.

"Be serious, Buck."

"I don't think it's healthy to be so damned serious."

And therein lies the fallacy of our relationship, Amie thought sadly, shifting uncomfortably to a cold spot on the leather seat. How much of what he'd said to her had he said to a dozen other women? How many times had he asked forgiveness when a woman's compliance suited his need for the moment? How many had he mesmerized with that voodoo charm of his?

"You were pretty damned serious when you accused me," she said, feeling her anger rise again.

"It was hard for me to believe you could be like that," he said, staring ahead. "That's why I was so scared. The way it looked, I was your best ticket to get what you wanted for all those poor, down-and-out people I've been so jealous of. And I still couldn't believe it. It was because I couldn't believe it that I was afraid I was a damned fool. Then, when I saw you tonight, I knew I'd been right about more than one thing."

"Right about what?"

"For one, you're not a user, Amie. And I'm a bigger fool than I ever thought I could be."

Her bottom lip quivered. "Why do you say that?"

"I damned near lost you, didn't I?"

Buck Cameron, vulnerable? She knew it wasn't easy for him to admit. She moved closer and laid her hand on his thigh.

"You hurt me," she said in a choked voice.

"I'm sorry."

His hand tightened on hers and for a minute she thought he might break her fingers. His grip relaxed when he drew her hand to his lips and kissed each fingertip.

"Buck, why did you say you were jealous of all the poor people I try to help?"

"I was afraid they were more important to you than I was."

"They're important, but not that important," she said, touched by his willingness to admit such an insecurity. She turned her hand so their palms touched, then wove her fingers through his. A fragile silence settled over them.

Buck nosed the car onto the winding road that led to his home. Only a slice of a moon followed them, but the stars were even brighter than Amie remembered them the first time she had traveled this road with Buck. They sparkled in a sky that seemed close enough to touch, and she cracked her window to smell the earthy, woodland fragrance that teased her senses and heightened passion's glow. She turned her face from the window, turned to see Buck's profile framed by the soft shadows within the car's interior.

"I know why you like it so much out here," she said when they suddenly left the forest for the softly rolling hills. "It's other-worldish. When you come out of the forest, it's like landing on another planet. Everyday life is left behind and you find yourself spellbound by the idea that here, in this separate place, there are no rules, no boundaries, no expectations imposed by yourself or anyone else."

A slow smile softened Buck's features. Amie could see his face more clearly now that they'd left the dark shadows of the forest, and she saw that his eyes revealed far more than anything she could read from his now-faint smile. In the plush interior of the car, Amie sat still, waiting for the response he was shaping in his mind.

"That's what I hoped to find here, Amie—everything you just described. I did at first. But then I'd come home to my Shangri-la only to discover that after a few days, a week, sometimes a little longer, something important was missing from my life. I didn't know where to look for it because I didn't know what it was.

"I went to the tallest mountaintops in Peru where, for a time, I'd think I'd found it. But then the restlessness would come back to haunt me, to drive me on. I looked for it in fast cars, fast planes—even fast sex," he said with a sound that might pass for laughter, and she remembered all the little remarks Claus had made earlier.

"When all that failed, I tried to find it in the world of finance, thinking my Dad surely possessed whatever *it* was, and that he must have found it there. It didn't take long for me to see that no two men find themselves in the same place or in the same way."

"But you never tried politics," Amie commented.

"No, darlin', and that's one place I didn't look. As I said, each to his own."

"Tom told me that Josiah served in the state legislature for a long time."

"He survived four different administrations," Buck said. "Two were under the Democrats."

The way he enunciated Democrats made Amie giggle. "To be a Democrat doesn't mean you have to be vermin," she said. "No more than to be a Republican."

"What it means, is the Republicans have to work all the harder to keep something in the treasury. Even with Dad fighting every step of the way, two new state welfare bills passed during the last Republican administration."

"I know. One of them helped fund Crisis House the first six months of its operation. That was a waste of the taxpayers' precious money, wasn't it?"

"I won't answer that if you promise not to mention politics for the next twenty-four hours."

Again they fell silent for a time and then Amie said, "I know you must have been proud tonight. I almost burst with pride, just knowing you."

"I'm not sure it was pride I felt."

"But your photography means a lot to you."

"When I developed my first film, I guess I was hooked."

"But not fulfilled."

"No. Not fulfilled." He was quiet for a little while, then said, "I was in Africa when I first got an inkling of what was missing in my life. One night I was sitting in front of a campfire with Claus and his wife. We'd spent over a week in Nairobi waiting for a van I'd ordered from Germany, and then a night at Narok on our way back to the Masai Mara game reserve. We were dead tired from traveling all day, and by the time we set up camp nobody was talking much. We just sat, watching the sun setting and the moon rising at the same time over the Siria Escarpment.

"As the night grew deeper, I watched the two of them grow closer until I knew I was totally separate and apart from them. I knew they were in a world of their own, at perfect peace with themselves and whatever they were thinking and feeling. I figured then that they had whatever it was I was looking for, and that I might as well give up on it."

The car came to a stop and Buck turned to Amie. "I resigned myself to the fact that I'd never find love, Amie. Not the kind I'd witnessed that night. Then I found you."

Amie felt hot tears burn her eyes. It sounded good.

Did it *ever* sound good! But was she buying? If she knew the price, could she afford to pay it?

She tried treading water—tried to free herself from the depths of his mesmeric blue eyes. But the harder she fought to stay afloat, the closer she found herself drawn to Buck—to his eyes, his tantalizing mouth—until she was totally immersed, willfully lost to his kiss.

The bed was big and wide, an island suspended in the heavens with stars swirling above and around them. Their lovemaking had been fierce, yet with a gentle overture that softened the urgency with which they first came together. Buck's need had been great; hers no less, fueled by her unresolved doubts demanding to be quieted by the act of intimate possession. She could still feel the pressure of his hands on her body, his greedy mouth, and was still overwhelmed by the power with which they had taken and given to each other.

"Your hair's grown," Buck said, catching a long tendril that cascaded over one breast. He pulled her head back, making the long curve of her neck and the swell of her breasts vulnerable to his searching lips. Now that their urgency had been met, their loving began again with a slow, gentle tempo and soft, sweet touches.

Lingering kisses probed inviting depths until rising passion would not be denied, and with a wild burst of sensation they rushed on their spiraling journey. Faster, faster Buck thrust inside her and she rose to meet him, thrust and counter-thrust. Digging her heels into his buttocks, she clutched his shoulders, felt her heart race to catch up with his, cried out his name, and soared past reality to become the center of exploding stars.

Long moments passed before Amie knew they were two separate entities and not still one. She felt Buck's hand smooth her damp brow, caress her shoulder, curve around her waist. With a long, shaky sigh, breathing became more normal, and with one leg locked around his thighs she cuddled against him.

"We're so-o-o good together, darlin'." His hand tightened at her waist and his chin nuzzled the top of her head.

"Ummm. We are, aren't we?" She kissed the shoulder that supported her head; reached for his hand that gave her so much pleasure and pressed her lips against its palm. His chest rose with long, deep breaths, and Amie closed her eyes to join him in another journey. The journey of blissful sleep.

Amie woke before dawn to find Buck sprawled half across her, half across the bed. One thing her lover was not was a neat sleeper, she thought, smiling as she admired the perfect landscape—the smooth, firm mounds of his buttocks, the valley along his spine that was formed by hard, well-developed muscles on each side. His legs were in a figure-four, and she thought how perfectly developed were the muscles of his calves and thighs. She wanted to touch him, to let her palms graze his strong shoulders, his arms, to brush the lock of hair from his cheek. But he was sleeping so deeply, so peacefully, she didn't want to do anything that would wake him.

Carefully, she slipped from the bed. Quietly, she gathered the clothes that had been shed with such haste, folded them neatly, and laid them across a chair. Then she let herself into the spa area that opened off the bedroom.

She stepped into the shower and turned on the hot water full blast. Closing her eyes, she lifted her face to the sharp needles of water and smiled, remembering the night she'd spent in Buck's arms . . . beneath him, on top of him, a part of him. Only when she felt a sudden draft did she lower her face and open her eyes.

"God, Amie, you're beautiful!" Buck said, closing the shower door. "Every time I look at your body it's like seeing it for the first time. It knocks me right off my feet." His voice was suddenly husky, and his hands drew an outline of her before he reached for the bar of soap.

Amie couldn't remember being more aware of his body, the lean, animal strength of him, with the muscles rippling beneath smooth, tanned skin. "You're beautiful, too," she said, allowing herself the pleasure of looking at him, at the perfect symmetry of his naked body that made her catch her breath with an almost uncontrollable sense of excitement. Rivulets of liquid mercury spread through her belly, the tops of her thighs, and between her legs.

He began to soap her all over, lifting strands of wet hair that clung to her shoulders and to her breasts. Caressing hands moved slowly, tantalizingly, then lingered between her thighs where the ache was unbearable. Squeezing her legs together, she trapped his hand.

"Don't you wear anything when you sunbathe?" she asked, drawing a finger down the center of his chest, then splaying her hand to feel the tight curl of hair there, and lower at his groin.

"Amie! You're a witch," he murmured hoarsely

when her fingers curled around his swollen penis. She'd learned just how to touch him, the way he liked it best, and he moaned softly as he moved his soapy hand to give her equal pleasure. A thrill chased through her when she felt him grow inside her hand, turgid flesh against her palm. And she gasped as he backed her against the wall, covered her hand with his, then guided himself between her thighs. Her breasts pressed against his chest and she nibbled his shoulder.

The bar of soap fell to the tiled floor when both his hands dug into the firm softness of her bottom, lifting her to accommodate their need. Both her arms went around his neck as her legs locked around his waist.

"Ah, Amie, love," he said as he teased between her legs. "I want to make love to you over and over, in every position, every way possible." His lips brushed hers before his tongue thrust inside her mouth, then out again, tantalizing, like the hard, pulsing movements he made toward the center of her need.

Her body strained against him, tingled, ached, and her mind was going crazy with his erotic murmurings whispered between short but hungry kisses. "I can't wait."

At last, his mouth closed over hers and she clung to it, responding fiercely as she tightened her legs about his waist, taking him deeply into her. Sharp needles of hot water heightened the sensation of having him inside her and their bodies sought relief from the crescendo of desire that threatened to burst out of control.

"Oh, Amie, love." The sound of his voice recalled passion spent. "You do things to me I never thought possible.'' His words were slightly slurred and his hands touched her wonderingly—her face, her hair, her neck and shoulders. He took a wash-cloth and drew it gently between her legs, then dropped it to the floor to let his hand caress where the cloth had been, gently, not trying to arouse her.

Amie leaned against him, knowing the streams of water that cascaded down her cheeks were not solely from the shower. Emotion overwhelmed her. Her fingers tightened on his shoulders, then curled around his neck. She could feel his life's blood coursing through his carotid vein, pulsing against her finger-tips. And inside her. She knew she had more than Buck Cameron's body inside her. And she'd always know he was there—inside her heart, her mind, her soul.

They dried each other with huge, warm terry tow-els, then reluctantly helped dress each other. Buck found an old pair of his sister-in-law's jeans for Amie and gave her one of his shirts. ''You look all of sixteen now,'' he teased. ''Come on and let me make breakfast. I need to build up your strength before I ravish you again.''

''*My* strength? What about yours?''

''Just looking at you gives me all the strength I need,'' he teased, taking her hand and holding it to the bulge that showed in his tight jeans.

Amie chuckled. ''Think you can rustle up some bacon and eggs in that kitchen of yours?''

Stranger, of course, had other ideas when he saw them come into the kitchen. ''Why don't you take him outside?'' Buck asked. ''I'll have everything ready when you get back.''

Stranger was more than happy to go outside with

Amie. It was a beautiful, clear May morning with the dew still sparkling on the slender blades of blue-green grass beyond the bricked terrace. A rainbow of azaleas edged the evergreens, and hundreds of bright flowered bulbs filled geometric beds Amie knew required careful tending.

The garden gave way to meadow, and Stranger ran ahead, dashing off into the edge of the wood to see what small, wild creature he could terrify. The sun was beginning to rise over the hill, and Amie hastened her pace, anxious to see what lay behind.

Not to be outdone, Stranger laid back his ears, glancing over his shoulder as he bounded ahead. Amie chased after him, flinging herself on the damp ground when she reached the top of the hill, ashamed she had to pant for breath.

At the bottom of the hill was a lush, green valley surrounded on all sides by a wood. At the edge of the north wood, water from a stream rushed over large boulders, and nestled in the southeast corner was a small cottage. Amie pushed herself up and started down the hill toward Stranger, who was standing in front of the cottage. His tail wagged with excitement.

As Amie approached, a man came through the screened front door. He wore faded overalls over a blue denim shirt. A hat with more character than most people have sat back on a shock of salt-and-pepper hair that curled over the tops of his ears. He was a man of small stature, but when Amie looked into his eyes she imagined the word small could be applied to him only in a physical sense.

She couldn't guess how old he was. His face was weathered, but his back was straight, and he was strong enough not to topple over backwards when

Stranger reared up and put both front paws against his chest.

"Mornin'," the man said, jamming one hand inside a pocket of his overalls while the other warded off Stranger's enthusiastic advances.

While his dark eyes seemed soft, Amie imagined they were sharp enough to see anything he took a notion to see. "You must be Luke," she said with a smile. "I'm Amie Phillips, a friend of . . . Stranger's." Somehow, she couldn't bring herself to mention Buck's name. This early in the morning it would be the same as admitting she'd spent the night with him. Because Luke appeared to be about the same age as her mother, she felt he might disapprove, and with one look into his eyes she knew his approval was important to her. Of course, she doubted she was the first woman that Luke might suspect had spent the night with Buck. Even so, she felt her cheeks grow hot. She wasn't used to being seen so early morning with the bloom of love newly on her face.

"Stranger don't make friends too easy," Luke said, taking a seat on the edge of his porch. "He's mighty particular 'bout who he likes and don't like." As he spoke, he seemed to be studying her. "He's a lot like his master," he added with an unexpected twinkle in his eyes.

"The air smelled so good out this morning," Amie said, "we decided to walk over the hill and see what was on the other side."

"One side's about the same as the other," Luke said, spitting a stream of something Amie guessed was tobacco. "Got a lonely old man on this side, and a lonely youngun on the other." With that, he looked off toward the tops of the pines that bounded the other side of the stream.

Amie found herself edging up to the porch and taking a seat on the bottom step near where Luke sat. She sat there, saying nothing, waiting for him to speak again.

"Maybe he won't be so lonely now," Luke said after a while.

"Why do you think he's been lonely?" Amie asked, thinking it was strange the way both of them were referring to Buck as *he*.

"Janie, my wife, passed on a few years back," the old man said, still gazing off through the tops of the pines. "Had two younguns that pneumonia took when they was both little. We was sharecroppers, Janie and me, and when she went, I just up and left myself—couldn't stay around a place we'd been together at so long. I happened up here one day asking for a little work, and been here ever since."

Luke fell silent and Amie waited to see what his poignant story had to do with Buck's being lonely or not. She knew Luke would tell her in his good time.

Luke spit again, then looked directly at Amie. "He understood how I felt." He nodded his head slowly. "He knew what I was about, and he understood. Unusual for a man so young." Again he nodded his head slowly, affirming his own thoughts. "His reasons are different from mine, but he's mighty restless, that one. And he's seen loneliness, face to face."

"But you don't know why? Why he's lonely, I mean. Luke, he told me once that he was never lonely."

Luke smiled. It was such a palpable smile that

Stranger felt its happy vibes and wagged his tail. "It's his nature," Luke said. "A man denies what he can't handle; like I wouldn't let myself believe for a long time that Janie was gone and wouldn't be coming back. Still don't believe it half the time," he admitted with an infectious chuckle. "Now, that one . . . ," he inclined his head toward the hill, ". . . he won't admit he's ailing 'til he's found the cure."

A light flickered in Luke's eyes and he put out his hand to pat Amie on the head, much as he had patted Stranger's.

"Stranger here . . .," Luke nodded toward the dog, ". . . he's never brought one of his friends around before." He took off his hat to scratch his head thoughtfully, then used it to smooth back his hair as he replaced it. "No, I can't say as how I've seen anything the likes of you around here. I'd say you could be just the cure he's been waitin' for."

"Don't go jumping to conclusions, Luke." Amie stood, took a deep breath, and stretched. As she readied to leave, she asked, "Do you take care of the gardens? They're really beautiful."

"I trim most of the hedges; keep the azaleas cut back. He does the rest, unless he's gone off someplace with that camera of his. Guess he'll be staying around more now that we've found you," he added with a wink and a tilt of his head.

Amie could smell bacon and strong coffee when she poked her head into the kitchen. "We didn't mean to take so long," she said when Buck turned to give her an admiring glance.

"You must have met Luke," he said with a broad grin.

"I'm sure that's who it was, though he never did

confirm that was his name.'' She slipped her arms around Buck's waist from behind, laying her cheek against his back. ''He did say that his wife's name was Janie, and he lives in the cottage in the valley. Was that Luke, or an apparition?''

''Both,'' Buck said, smiling as he turned the bacon. He reached for a dishcloth and wiped the grease spatters from the top of the stove, giving Amie a curious glance as he crushed the cloth into a little ball and tossed it into the sink. ''He told you about his wife?''

''Umhum. He still misses her a lot, doesn't he?''

''I know he must, but he never talks about her. When he first came here, he told me she was dead. He's never mentioned her since then. That's why it seems unusual that he'd tell you about her.''

''You know me, Buck. I go around collecting hearts to wear with the big one on my sleeve.''

He set the pan of bacon aside and turned to gather her into his arms. ''All I know is that you have mine, darlin',' he said in a husky voice.

Amie ate slowly, watching Buck from across the table. He seemed happy this morning—quietly loving and content. She smiled when he buttered a fourth piece of toast. He'd made a country breakfast—a big plate of scrambled eggs, bacon, and a pot of southern grits. And he was eating like a farmhand!

''I'm glad Barbara left some of her clothes here,'' Buck said. ''I believe those are Mother's sneakers, though. Barb has big feet.''

Amie grinned. ''Buck, it's perfectly natural that you'd have women's clothes here. I'm sure somebody's always forgetting something.''

He gave her a smile. ''When I'm out of town, Barbara and Mom come over to use the spa. Dad and Wicket are too cheap to install one. Mother has a jacuzzi only because the doctor told her it would be good for her arthritis, so Dad was able to deduct it as a medical expense.'' He laughed, shaking his head.

He finished his coffee and took the cup and saucer to the sink. Then he came to stand behind Amie, putting his hands on her shoulders. ''You wouldn't consider bringing Charlie and Brigette and moving in with me, would you?''

''No.''

''You don't like the idea.''

''No, I don't like the idea.''

His thumbs plied the taut muscles at the base of her neck, then his fingers threaded upward through her hair, massaging her scalp. ''You wouldn't care to elaborate on that, would you?'' His question was tentative, his words faltering. ''Maybe I could shoot a hole in your reasoning.''

''I don't think so,'' Amie replied.

''You don't?''

''No.''

''I love you, darlin'.''

Her heart became a throbbing, thumping mass. ''And I love you,'' she said softly. ''It's just that . . .''

''I know,'' he said, ''you don't know what you'd tell Lizbeth.''

''No, dammit,'' she said, turning on him. ''Lizbeth has nothing to do with it. If I wanted to move in with you, I would. But I don't.''

He had known, somehow, that it wouldn't work when he asked her. He asked anyway, hoping. He wished he could offer her more, but at the moment that was impossible. ''I thought if we could spend more time together . . .''

Amie waited for him to finish his sentence, but he didn't. His words trailed off into nothingness.

"Time isn't going to change either of us, Buck. Not in the way you mean. And I know love isn't always enough to make a relationship work. The only thing my moving in here would do is make us see what we already know—that we're different in very basic ways."

Amie knew the game was up. For her, it had been a long time ago. "Love's a serious thing for me," she said. "It means all the things you've avoided all your adult life, I imagine. The kind of love I'm talking about has enough strings attached to it to weave a whole life, Buck. It's the whole ball of yarn, including children and a lifetime commitment."

Conflicts that she couldn't begin to decipher played over his face. "I should tell you," she said, "if anyone's been deceitful, I have. You've never made a secret of who and what you are. I thought I could play your game, but now I know I can't. I'm ready to admit now that I'm way out of your league when it comes to love. Do you think I don't know you couldn't be happy settling down with one woman?" She met his clouded expression with crystal clear eyes.

"How can you be so sure of that?"

"Because if you could, I doubt I'd be here now. You'd have that Peruvian woman here."

Had she actually said it? She felt giddy as the blood seemed to drain from her face. She wanted to look away from the stunned expression on his face, but she didn't. She forced herself to watch the gathering storm.

TWELVE

"What in hell are you talking about, Amie?"

The sharpness of his voice cut deeper, hurt more than an actual blow might have.

"I'm sorry," she said. "It's none of my business."

"You just made it your business. And whoever told you, she made it hers, too. It was Marsha, wasn't it? My mother must have told her."

Amie spun around to reply, but his expression stopped her. It was more than anger that darkened his eyes, tightened his features to give his face a mask-like quality.

"*Wasn't* it?"

"What difference does it make who told me? It's true, isn't it?"

His expression alarmed her. It kept changing, subtle changing, like the first stirrings of dangerous storm clouds, the prelude to devastation.

"There's something you need to know about me, Amie, and you might as well learn it now . . . and learn it well."

She held her breath, wondering how she could have thought she knew anything at all about Buck Cameron. Was this the man she thought she loved? She cringed, knowing it wouldn't surprise her if he struck her.

"There are some things in my life that I consider private . . . not to be touched. If you can't have a little faith . . ."

"*Faith*? You're telling me to have faith when . . ."

"I'm telling you that without it . . ."

"*Blind* faith, at that," she shouted incredulously. "For me, it takes a leap of faith to embrace my religion. And you, Buck Cameron, are not God, even if you tend to think so at times."

His eyes narrowed. He whirled away to stride quickly across the room. In seconds he was at the door that led down to the garage. He opened it with such force, Amie thought he'd surely jerk the knob off. He slammed it so hard behind him the crystal goblets jangled against each other in the cabinet and made discordant, tinkling sounds.

Stranger whimpered, then barked, close at Amie's heels as she ran across the kitchen. She flung open the door and saw the Mercedes still parked, but heard the Jaguar's motor revving.

"Don't you dare leave me here like this," she shouted. But Buck's only reply was a cloud of exhaust as the car shot backward, then spun around the parking circle and zoomed out of sight.

Stranger reared up, almost knocking Amie down. With a plaintive whimper, he licked her across the face. Amie leaned against the door, raised her hand to wipe the tears from her cheeks. She wasn't certain where they came from . . . the tears.

* * *

It was almost dusk when Amie stepped from the taxi onto the concrete sidewalk in front of her apartment. For a while she'd waited at Buck's, wondering if a call would come from some nameless voice to say Buck had wrapped himself around a tree, or worse. She'd stopped trying to guess why he'd reacted so violently, so unreasonably. What had he said? *There are some things in my life I consider private . . . not to be touched.*

And what did faith have to do with it? She let him know that she knew about the woman in Peru, and he made no attempt to deny it. Instead, he accused her of intruding on his privacy, and had the gall to accuse her of having no faith in him. None of it made sense.

The phone was ringing inside when she opened the door. "Amie?" she heard before she could even say hello.

Somehow she'd known it was Buck. "Yes?" she answered quietly.

"Amie, I'm sorry. God, I'm so sorry. I'm sorry I lost control . . . sorry I left you like that."

For a minute she just sat there, unable to speak. She was so tired . . . numb.

"Amie?"

"I've been so worried . . ." She paused, a little in awe of her admission. She should be *angry*, not worried.

"I know you won't believe it, and I can understand why . . . God, I really can understand why . . . but it's going to be all right. I'm going to make it right for us. Will you try to believe that?"

"Buck, where are you?"

"Please don't ask me to explain anything right now, darlin'. Do that one thing for me and I'll spend the rest of my life doing everything I can to make you happy. I'll explain everything, to your full satisfaction, when I get back."

"And when will that be?"

"Toward the end of the week."

"The *end* of the *week*?"

"Easy, darlin', easy. I swear to God it's going to be all right. Just listen to me right now. Okay?"

Silence.

"I called the house but nobody answered. I don't have time now to get in touch with Luke, so if you'll tell him I'll be gone for a while, it'll be a big help."

"I wouldn't have left Stranger without telling Luke," she said, tempted to add that just rushing off and leaving even a dog stranded was not her way of doing things.

"Amie?" His voice was very soft, very low.

"Yes?"

"I love you."

The tears were flowing freely down her cheeks now, and she took a tissue from a container near the phone to wipe her nose.

"I'll call you when I get back," Buck said into the silence.

"Where *are* you?"

"Houston. I have to go now, darlin'. I love you."

"I knew this day would come," Anna Maria said quietly and without dramatics. She sat in the middle of the bed with her legs crossed, yoga-style, and began to brush her long hair. One smooth, sunbrowned shoulder escaped from the bright yellow peasant blouse she wore. "You've taken care of me long enough, Buck, so don't . . . is the word *fret*? . . . yes, don't fret, Buck."

He laughed softly. The way she pronounced his name, *Book*, always amused him. So young, he thought, as he stood looking at her. So damned young to have been through so much. "I don't intend to abandon you, Anna Maria," he said with a tender smile.

"You have been so good to me," she said almost as a reprimand. "You have given me far more than I could ever give you. You gave me life, Buck Cameron. If not for you, I would have died . . . and a terrible death, at that."

A dark cloud passed over her face, but then it was gone and she laughed, her eyes growing bright. "Such a bad hombre you were," she said in a voice filled with pride. "Anna Maria can walk through any village now, knowing she will not be harmed. Not only that, she can walk with pride, with her head held high. Everyone knows the powerful American takes care of her."

"Don't do that, Anna Maria. You know I don't like it when you revert to third person to speak of yourself." He hadn't missed the veil of memory that had blown across her face.

"I'm sorry for using . . . third person, you say? Sometimes I forget." She watched him intently while offering a smile. "You are thinking about our time together, are you not?"

"Yes," he answered with a smile of his own. "I remember how happy you were . . . like a small child . . . when I bought this place and moved you into it. It's yours now, you know," he reminded her. "And all the land behind, up to the top of the mountain where the stars come down at night."

Rising on her knees, she placed her hands on his shoulders and began to knead. "You're always so tense when you come here,'' she said, her voice soft, reflecting gratitude.

''But not so much when I leave,'' he said, letting his head drop against his chest so her fingers could better ply their magic.

''I owe you so much,'' Anna Maria said fervently. ''I will never be able to repay you.''

''Seeing you with Ramond in your arms gives me more happiness than a man deserves,'' he said. He turned to her, taking both of her hands and clasping them between his.

Stupid. He'd been stupid to tell Wicket and his mother about Anna Maria. He should have known his mother couldn't keep a secret from Marsha. And he could just imagine what those two women thought about Ramond. Dammit. He would not have this part of his life . . . Anna Maria's life . . . reduced to gossip. He would not have her name slandered. He felt a rising fury when he thought anyone, and especially Marsha, would dare imply that Anna Maria was a kept woman. What did Marsha or anyone else know about her? And to tell Amie . . .

''No more thoughts that make your face grow dark,'' said Anna Maria. ''Let me talk to you about Ramond. This always puts a smile on your face.''

''Yes,'' Buck said to her. ''Tell me about Ramond.''

Anna Maria smiled, looking at him from beneath her lashes. ''He has a new friend,'' she said tentatively. ''Tomas.''

Rising, Buck drew her from the bed. ''Let's go find Ramond and his nanny. On the way, you can tell me all about Tomas.''

* * *

What happened to you and Buck last Saturday night?'' Marsha asked Amie. ''Caroline was beside herself. She couldn't believe he'd left his opening.''

Though Marsha didn't add *with you*, Amie knew it was what she meant. ''I left before Buck did,'' she said.

''You did? Claus said you left together.''

And who said women were the only ones who couldn't keep their mouths closed? ''In a manner of speaking, but only after I called a taxi for myself.'' Amie wondered why she was bothering to defend her actions to Marsha.

''For the two of you to be so cozy, he must have come clean about the woman in Peru.''

''That's none of my business, Marsha.''

''No? Then you must not be serious about Buck. If you were, you couldn't be so understanding about another woman, especially when there's a child.''

Amie held her breath, then let it out slowly. *A child*?

When Amie said nothing, Marsha merely lifted her brows. ''Oh, well. If you don't want to talk about it . . . What are you doing for lunch?''

Amie felt a smug satisfaction from not rising to Marsha's bait, but she had to cut their conversation short, or else she'd betray herself. ''I told Whitney Crawford I'd meet him for lunch at the Tower.''

''Whitney Crawford? What are you seeing him about?''

''I'm not sure,'' she said. ''He asked me to lunch, that's all.''

''Ummm, that's interesting,'' Marsha said, eyeing Amie curiously. As she left for her own office, she glanced back over her shoulder.

Amie pretended not to notice the question in Marsha's eyes. *A child.* She knew she had to get control of herself. She had a luncheon appointment, and then she had to decide what to do with the rest of her life.

As long as she lived, she'd never forget how she felt when Whitney Crawford said, ever so casually, "I talked with Buck Cameron this morning. He called from Peru. Looks like we're going to get that land you've had your eye on, after all."

At least she managed to make Crawford believe her stunned reaction was due to her being overjoyed. Little did he know she had no idea what Buck had been up to, and certainly not that he was in Peru. Houston, he'd said. What had he hoped to gain by lying to her?

Now that she knew a child was involved, she wondered what he could possibly have meant when he said he was going to make everything right for them. Did he think he could wipe out a couple of lives as easily as a chalked lesson on a blackboard?

She couldn't say her time in Charlotte was totally in vain. She supposed Buck decided to sell that downtown property to the city to ease his conscience where she was concerned. What difference did it make? The important thing was that now her dream for the homeless would be realized. Not only would there be space for some low-income housing, but according to the architect and the developer, plenty of room for a good-sized shelter. As for Buck, he could stay in Peru for all she cared. From all indications, it was where he belonged.

"What will I do here without you?" Marsha actually seemed upset. "I honestly feel that we're friends now, and I hate the thought of you leaving."

"My leaving has nothing to do with you, Marsha."

"But it's so sudden. Everything seemed fine when you left for lunch. What happened?"

"Actually, lunch was very productive," Amie said without emotion of any kind. "I've explained that."

"All you've told me is that Whitney Crawford said the commission could go ahead with that project you've been working on. The one you didn't tell me about," she added pointedly.

"And that's all there is to tell. My work on the project is in the file I gave you."

She wished she could give Marsha an explanation, but she couldn't. Right now she couldn't even tell Millie. She didn't want to think about it, much less discuss it. All she was certain of was that she had to leave Charlotte. She knew how it would seem to Millie. She'd accuse her of running away again. But she couldn't help that. This was not the same as it had been with Joe. All she'd wanted was a new start when she came to Charlotte. This time, it was to save a life . . . her own.

"Do you have another job?" Marsha asked. "What are you going to do?"

"I applied for a teaching position in the Moore County district before I heard about the opening here. They seemed disappointed when I turned down their offer—with the shortage of teachers everywhere, you know—so I'm going to call them this afternoon. Of course, I'll have to wait 'til the end of this semester even if they do have an opening, but that isn't very long. The truth is, I could use a little time to myself. I have a little money saved, so if I can manage to get a contract in my hands for next semester, I can use the time until then to settle into an apartment and get used to the place."

"And you think you'll be happy doing that?"

I'll be happy when I make love to you. "Teaching is more in line with my training. A master's in sociology, I've decided, is better suited for the classroom."

"You love your work here," Marsha insisted. "It's because of Buck, isn't it?"

Amie cut Marsha a hard glance.

"I'd like to clear something up, Amie. I don't want you leaving without understanding why I've said so many ugly things about Buck."

"Marsha, forgive me, but right now I couldn't care less how you feel about Buck."

But Marsha persisted. "Has he told you anything about Charles, except that he died in Kenya?" Marsha asked.

"Yes. He said you blame him for your husband's death."

"Charles always liked to hunt—deer, mostly," Marsha said. "We knew Buck was familiar with the areas in Africa where hunting is allowed, and time and again Charles tried to persuade him to take us with him on his trips. He kept refusing until Caroline finally joined in the effort. She told him Charles and I were like family, and she couldn't believe he wouldn't share his knowledge of the country with us. I think she may even have used the word selfish."

Amie winced, knowing that must have hurt Buck.

Marsha slipped down from the desk and walked to the window. "I won't burden you with the whole story, but I'd like to tell you a few things Buck probably left out. I guess I owe it to him and to myself to admit the truth at last." Amie made no comment. "Everything went wrong from the beginning," Marsha continued. "Charles and I insisted on staying at one of the modern tourist hotels, and Buck balked at that. He was used to living out of his van and preferred the solitude that couldn't be found where so many people gathered.

"The worst of it was the hunting itself. Neither of us realized how strongly Buck felt about killing the animals, and we didn't believe him when he kept telling us we'd be on our own when we got there. Once we saw he meant it, we both panicked. Buck talked to a group that was planning a safari outside the Mara, and persuaded them to let us join them. Then he loaded his equipment into his van and took off on his own, agreeing to meet us back at Little Governor's Camp two weeks later."

Marsha walked out of the room without a word, then came back with a cup of coffee. "The accident . . . Three days before we were to meet Buck, Charles was run down in an elephant stampede."

"Marsha, are you all right?" Amie asked, seeing the terror in her eyes the memory evoked.

"I think I am—at last." Marsha paused as if to reaffirm the statement she'd made. "I wasn't the only one to lose a husband that day. Two others in the safari met with the same fate. Their wives recognized what had happened. They knew the men had acted foolishly, had gotten too close, had shot when they shouldn't have, and started the stampede. But me, I didn't see it that way. I blamed Buck. I told him it wouldn't have happened if he'd been with Charles, and that he should have been, knowing Charles's inexperience. I said he might as well have pushed Charles in front of those elephants."

"Oh, Marsha . . ." How unfair that Buck should be given such a burden when none of the fault was his.

"I know," Marsha said sorrowfully. "It was an

awful thing for me to do. But I needed to blame someone, Amie, and Buck was there, trying to make things easier for me, yet I turned on him. It's been very awkward, too, since then, with me being so close to Caroline and the rest of the family. Caroline and Wick have a wonderful relationship, but until he retired from his active role in politics, there were times when she admitted her loneliness to my mother. Wicket and Barbara were in Washington a lot of the time, and you know Buck. He was always out there chasing a tiger's tail."

. . . And you know Buck. I thought I did. I don't always understand him, but I thought I knew him.

"Amie?"

"I'm sorry. Something you said made me lose my train of thought. You were talking about Caroline being lonely."

"Yes, that's how she and Mother became so close. Then, soon after Charles was killed, my mother died, and Caroline took me under her wing. She didn't turn her back on me even though I was accusing her son, and I know there were times when that was difficult."

"Yes, I can see how that could be," Amie said.

"I'm ashamed to admit it, Amie, but for the longest time I've done everything I could to hurt Buck, thinking it would ease some of my own hurt. Of course, it never did."

Amie wished it was in her heart to say something kind, but at the moment she simply didn't feel that big hearted.

"I even lied to Buck about you," Marsha said, looking at Amie uncomfortably. "When you left early to go over to Millie's, I told him . . ."

"I know about that, Marsha," Amie interrupted.

"I didn't say anything to you because it worked out okay. He called my mother, then figured out for himself that you'd . . ."

"Lied."

"Yes."

"I'd like to make it up to both of you. I know Buck loves you. You're the first woman he's ever taken to his parents' home."

"Dinner with the folks isn't exactly a commitment, Marsha."

"Whatever happened between you must have upset him, too, or he wouldn't have left town like that. One Christmas right after Charles was killed I caused an awful scene in front of his family. Caroline took my side and the next morning Buck left for Peru and was gone for weeks."

That must have been the time he left his Christmas tree up so long, Amie thought, remembering that he said it was a bad time for him. "I'm glad you confided in me, Marsha," she said, "but as far as Buck and I are concerned, we're too different in too many ways to have a lasting relationship."

"Nothing I've said has changed your mind about leaving?"

"No," Amie said. "But I think you should tell Buck how you feel now. If you owe anyone anything, you owe him that."

When Amie woke Friday morning, everything ached: her muscles, from getting her furniture ready to be packed onto the moving van; her bones, from tossing and turning all night; and her heart. She was not happy about leaving Charlotte.

She reminded herself again that Rockingham had its compensations. Of primary importance was the fact that she would be only half an hour from Lizbeth . . . and there would be nothing there to remind her of Buck.

She dressed in her jeans and the blue cotton shirt she'd left folded on a chair, fed Charlie and Brigette, drank the last of the orange juice, and went over her list of things that had to be done before she could leave. Everything was in order. She'd given the movers a key to the apartment, lined up the clean-up crew and paid them in advance, packed the car with the few things she would need in case the cats became rowdy, and . . . She checked off the last item: call Mother.

She had called Lizbeth the night before, thank heavens. Her ears were still burning from her mother's fiery tongue-lashing. Up to the last minute, Lizbeth refused to believe Amie was going through with her plans to leave Charlotte. Until last night her mother had listened, but refused to hear what Amie was saying. Now she'd have to accept it as fact, and get used to the idea that her daughter might never marry.

When both cats were in their carriers, Amie checked her purse. All her credit cards were there, the key to the beach house she had rented for two weeks until her lease on the new apartment began, a small amount of cash in case of an emergency, and . . . what was that?

She plucked a three-cornered piece of paper from the bottom of her purse. Buck Cameron, in her own scrawling penmanship, was written in fading letters on the scrap of paper. Below his name was his office address. She had scribbled it down the first day she'd gone there to persuade him to make a donation to Crisis House. Almost four months ago. It was such a short time, a remarkably short time; yet it seemed a lifetime ago. And it was. *My* lifetime, Amie thought, letting the paper slip from her fingers. She watched it flutter to the floor, stood staring at it for a moment, then took the handle of a kitty carrier into each hand and shouldered her way through the front door, pushing it shut with her foot. "You may as well settle down in there," she chided Brigette. "You have a lot farther to go than to the car."

The car sputtered when she turned it on and pressed the accelerator. It had never done that. Only after several tries did she get it to start, but this didn't surprise her. "Not even the car wants to go," she muttered, laughing when Charlie gave a plaintive meow. She drove to the corner and waited for an opening in the traffic. Then, spinning the steering wheel, she pressed the accelerator and shot forward. Not once did she look back.

THIRTEEN

Amie didn't bother to ask herself what she was doing when she turned onto the little dirt road that was closed away from the world by a deep wood on each side. Deep down, she knew that ever since Whitney Crawford told her Buck was in Peru, she'd known she couldn't leave without one last look at the place where she'd touched the stars.

With the windows down, she could smell the promise of a long, hot summer in the air. When the forest ended abruptly and her car burst into the sunlight, she saw white ducks making rippling patterns on the surface of the lakes she passed. Shimmering ripples, like the memories of her mind: dappled sunlight on white, rumpled sheets. Morning in the meadow when Stranger raced her up the hill. The rich scent of coffee, the taste of Buck's mouth, shivers up her spine. All these, she was leaving behind.

But never mind, she thought. She'd known that wondrous meadow, the rumpled sheets, the taste of

Buck's mouth, and more. She'd touched the stars, ridden on the tail of a comet, split the white-hot center of the moon. She'd had it all.

So never mind, Amie. Never mind that no other lifetime will ever be the same, will ever be so sweet, so filled with happiness, with the joy of loving.

And what are you looking for, Amie? What, exactly, do you want?

I want to be happy.

I'll be happy when I make love to you.

For just an instant Amie stopped breathing. Then her breath came with great gulps of air. Her heart forgot its tempo and raced madly out of time. Her foot hit the brakes. She knew she was caught in the eye of a storm.

A tall man stood at the edge of the wood. A big, shaggy dog stood beside him. The dog barked. The man ran his fingers through his thick, windblown hair. Amie knew that if she were close enough, she'd be able to see his eyes that were bluer than the sky.

She turned off the motor and sat clutching the steering wheel, looking through her windshield at the man and his dog. The sun was bright. The man put his hand up to shield his eyes. He stood, returning her gaze though she knew he couldn't see her eyes. If he could, he'd know they were blurred, that she could see only the shape of him now as he lowered his hand and made long strides toward her.

The dog followed at his heels. When they covered exactly half the distance between the wood and Amie's car, the man stopped. He held out his hand to stay the dog. Its tail wagged, then it bent its hind legs and sat beside its master.

It seemed he stood there for an eternity, and Amie

sat behind the wheel of her car. Then he jammed his hands into his pockets, pulling the tight jeans he wore tautly across his slender hips. He cocked his head to one side. The dog cocked its head to the same side.

Amie pried her fingers from the steering wheel and opened the door of her car. She stepped outside.

Slowly, tentatively, she began the walk that would cover the distance between them. He had come half-way, and the other half was hers. It was no more than fifty yards, but it may as well have been fifty miles for all the effort it took her to take the first five steps. But then it became easier. Her pace quickened and her feet moved swiftly. She stopped short, leaving a space of five feet that she felt she needed permission to close.

"Amie."

Only her name, and no more. But never had her name sounded so sweet. It was a melody that curled through her mind, warmed her heart, touched her with unbidden hope.

"You told me you were in Houston," she said, smiling nervously.

"I was," he said quietly. "Now I've come home."

Whatever he was thinking or feeling, Amie couldn't begin to guess. Did his eyes hold surprise? Curiosity? Mere indifference, perhaps? He didn't ask what she was doing there. She didn't tell him why she'd come.

The blue shirt he wore was buttoned only at the bottom. A summer breeze flirted through his hair, crept under one side of his shirt, making it billow, and the brush of hair on his deeply tanned chest caught soft rays of the sun.

If only he would hold out his arms, she thought; if only he would say something else—anything. The spring of her heart had been wound too tight and her pulse was racing out of control. She tried to breathe deeply, only to discover her breath was choppy, her lungs about to collapse. Was it possible that neither of them would ever move again? Would people come from everywhere to see the statues of a man, his dog, and a woman who was separated from them by a distance of five feet? Five feet, Amie thought. Only five feet between me and the rest of my life.

But what of her doubts? What about Peru and the woman Marsha had said waited for him there? What about his reaction when she'd asked him about it? And there was the child . . .

How many times had she been over it in her mind? His initial anger seemed to be directed at Marsha. While he had denied nothing, he'd told Amie he loved her. And there was the call from Houston. At least he'd said it was Houston. But he was here now, not in Peru. What had he said? *Now I've come home.*

If only she could be sure . . . if only she could know if life waited five feet away . . . or merely a mirage. She took a tentative step forward.

Stranger leapt from Buck's side, making Amie stagger when his two front feet landed on her shoulders. His big, wet tongue lapped at her face.

"He's telling you that he missed you," Buck said. "Luke was asking for you, too."

Subduing Stranger, Amie dared to look up at Buck. "What about you?" she asked quietly, risking his rejection.

"I see your car's packed. What does that mean?"

So what did she expect? She noted he hadn't budged an inch from where he stood. "It means I've decided to leave Charlotte.'' She saw a flash of emotion in his eyes—perhaps nothing more than curiosity.

''What you really mean is that you've decided to leave me.''

There was a rustling of leaves, and her hand brushed at a wisp of hair the breeze blew across her eyes. ''I'm sorry,'' she said. ''I wouldn't have come if I'd known you were here.''

''You wouldn't have?''

She inched her foot another step forward. ''No. I don't like intruding on you like this.''

He gave her a long, searching look that made her want to cry out, to tell him she couldn't help herself—that she had to come, had to have some measure of communion with him this one last time. And that even though she had thought he was thousands of miles away, she'd felt there was so much of him here, so much of what he was, she would be able to touch his presence, feel his spirit . . .

She stepped forward again, shortening the distance between them. If she held out her hand, she could almost touch him. Still, Buck didn't move.

What to do? Her mind grasped for possibilities. What if she didn't take the risk? From nowhere came a sudden thought. *The hand of love will lead you.* She'd never heard those words before. Perhaps they were an answer to her prayers. Perhaps the magic of words was out there all the time, part of the energy of the universe, waiting to be tapped by the subconscious.

She looked at Buck's feet planted firmly in place. He hadn't moved an inch beyond the halfway mark. If she didn't cross that mark, could she risk wondering for the rest of her life about what might have been?

She looked up and saw his eyes following the movement of hers. When she saw a lazy smile begin to soften his features, she knew he was reading her mind again. His hands reached across the distance between them to rest lightly on her shoulders. She took the final step and felt herself enclosed in the circle of his arms.

"It took you a damned long time to meet me halfway," he said in a choked voice.

Amie muffled her sob. "I wasn't sure if that was what you wanted, or if you meant for me to stay on my side of the line."

"I got in late last night, so Luke came over and made breakfast for me this morning. Have you eaten, or did you have only orange juice and coffee?"

"I'm not here for breakfast, Buck. I'm in the process of moving."

He made his exasperation clear. "What in hell am I supposed to do, Amie? Do you think I didn't hear you? I did—loud and clear. So is this supposed to be a good-bye hug? Or what?"

Or what? Her bottom lip trembled and she could only shake her head.

He turned her, tightening one arm around her shoulders. "Charlie and Brigette will be fine with your windows down. Let's go to the house, Amie. I think it's time we settled a few things. One, in particular."

Buck heaped Amie's plate with bacon, eggs, a hot biscuit and jam. "This should be enough to keep your mouth busy while I talk," he said with a disarming grin. "No interruptions. Agreed?"

She nodded.

"Almost three years ago," he began, "I was in a small Peruvian village and at such odds with myself I could find no peace. It wasn't late, and I knew I'd never get to sleep if I tried, so I decided to go for a walk. The village is very small and for the people who live there—except for a few affluent foreigners who discovered, as did I, that it's a great place to run away to—the water supply is a common well. A small dirt road—more a path, actually—leads down to the well, and that's the direction I took.

"Just before I reached the well I heard muffled cries. At first I thought a jaguar had taken one of the villager's goats, but as I drew closer to the sound I realized it was not the cry of an animal."

Amie put down her fork, overcome by the pained expression on Buck's face. And there was anger. A thin white line etched his mouth and his eyes flashed blue fire.

"I was never without a pistol, in case I was forced to defend myself against a hungry animal. Until then, it had never occurred to me that the most dangerous animal of all was my own species."

He pushed back from the table and Amie saw his clenched fists.

"There were three men," he said, "renegades from another village, and one was raping a young girl while the other two waited their turns."

"My God, Buck!" Amie gasped.

"I tried to rescue her, but they had knives," he said coldly. "Being the cowards they were, one ran away—fortunately for me. The one holding her down was killed when we fought, and the other badly wounded. I took the girl, Anna Maria, back to my room and found the closest thing to a doctor the village had. I called the authorities in the nearest city and reported the incident. No charges were pressed against me, and the wounded man is in prison now.

"Anna Maria had no family to speak of . . . girl babies born to poverty-stricken parents are a cheap commodity there.

"I found decent living quarters for Anna Maria and kept close tabs on her. When I realized she was pregnant, I told Mother and Wicket, explaining that I intended to take care of her and her baby, since she had no one else."

Overwhelmed, Amie found herself ecstatic and heartbroken by turns. How could she have doubted him? Why hadn't she trusted him when she knew he had trouble admitting he was an honorable man? She'd been too quick to believe Marsha's insinuations, when Marsha obviously didn't know the facts.

"Amie," Buck said, leveling his gaze at her. "There has never been anything between me and Anna Maria except a near father-daughter relationship. Because I know she was never used to kindness, I made it clear from the beginning that I expected no favors in return for rescuing her.

"When I realized Mother had told Marsha just enough to fire her imagination, I was furious—not with Mother, because Marsha's been someone for her to talk to and I should have expected as much. I was upset with myself. I know I've used Anna Maria and Ramond. Not intentionally, I swear. But for almost three years she, and then the two of them, have been there for me to take care of, to give some purpose to my life."

When he saw her meaningful smile, he sighed. "Hell, Amie. Who's to say who's deserving and who's not? Maybe I've learned something from this."

Still, she said nothing, only gave him her silent, though palpable support.

"When I called you from Houston," Buck continued, "I'd decided it was time I encouraged Anna Maria to take charge of her own life, and her son's. With a little help from her Uncle Buck, of course. I can't have them thinking I've abandoned them, but she needs a husband and Ramond needs a real father, just as I need . . ." Amie melted from his heated gaze when he paused to look at her as if he meant to devour her. ". . . as I need you, darlin'."

He took her hands and squeezed them, then held them while he talked. Willingly, she plunged into the depths of his deep blue eyes.

"In Houston, I saw an attorney. He's an old friend I use when I want to make certain no one in Charlotte learns my business. Anna Maria will be given a certain amount of money each month until she's married, and then she'll get a lump sum for her dowry. We also set up a trust fund for the boy, so his education will be assured."

Buck smiled for the first time since he'd been talking. "When I went to Peru to tell Anna Maria about you and the financial arrangements I've made for her and the boy, she told me about a young British astronomer, Tomas, who spends a lot of time there. It seems they've become close, and she says Ramond really likes him." He chuckled. "That dowry may come in handy sooner than I'd thought."

At last Amie felt she could speak. "Buck Cameron," she murmured, "you're more a softie than I ever realized. A wonderful one, I might add."

He found her lips and silenced her. Then, before she could speak again, he asked, "What about your furniture? Have you shipped it off to wherever you thought you were going?''

''The movers were picking it up this morning,'' she said, feeling he wanted to change the subject.

''I don't like doing this, darlin', but I have to ask you something.''

Darlin'. A Sousa march couldn't hold a candle to the rhythm of her thundering heart. Whatever he was about to ask, she had to have the right answer.

''What, exactly, *are* you doing here?''

Buck's eyes were riveted on her face. He sat very still, holding her, waiting.

''You damned fool,'' she blurted out, ''I'm in love with you!''

He rose to his feet, taking her with him. ''Say that again,'' he said quietly. With a widening smile he added, ''Not the damned fool bit, the other part.''

''I love you. I'll always love you. And this house, this separate place—the forest and the meadows and the softly rolling hills, and the clean, pure air—I knew it was all you and that even if you weren't here I'd be close to you.''

The tears in his eyes made them bluer than blue. ''Oh, Amie, my love, my darlin'. He kissed the lids of her eyes, then her cheeks. ''I love you, too,'' he said hoarsely as his mouth claimed hers.

He was her man. Only hers. She knew that now, and that they'd have a lifetime to discover new fields of wonder. Her arms tightened around him and she could feel the muscles in his broad chest meet the pressure of her straining breasts. Her tongue captured his in a fiery dance of passion and love, and her fingers dug into the hard flesh of his shoulders when his hands moved down and over the curves her tight jeans amplified.

At Stranger's loud, excited barking, they reluctantly drew apart. "My cats!" Amie cried. "Stranger's after Charlie and Brigette!"

Together, they dashed through the front of the house and down the drive. Stranger's head and front legs had disappeared through the back window of Amie's car and his tail was wagging furiously. Loud hisses issued from the two carriers on the backseat and two yellow paws, claws extended, slapped through the wire openings.

"Stranger!" Buck shouted. The dog slid from the window and down to the ground as if he were made of melted rubber. With his two front paws, he hid his face.

Buck turned to Amie with a big grin. "Well, I guess we have a whole new set of differences to grapple with here. I'll counsel my dog, if you'll talk some sense to your cats. But first, we'll have to call the movers so they can radio the van that picked up your things and turn them around before they get too far."

"Radio . . . ? Hold on a minute. What do you mean, before they get too far?"

"You don't mean to leave Charlotte now?"

"I've given up my job, Buck. Charlie and Brigette have ravenous appetites, and they won't eat any old cat food. And I've a contract with the Richmond County board of education."

"Have you signed it?"

"Well, no, but . . ."

His brows shot upward. "There's that three-letter word!"

"I have an obligation," she said weakly.

"You sure as hell do," he said, locking his arms around her waist. "We have an obligation to love each other, and we're not going to do it long distance.'' He was pressing his very masculine body against her and getting exactly the response he was aiming for. ''Do you hear me, Amie? I'm a hard man to deal with.''

A silly, lopsided grin took control of her face. What the hell? She leaned into him and whispered against his ear. ''Yeah, so I notice. And I can't wait to do something about that.''

His kiss was everything she'd been dreaming about and, in true Buck Cameron fashion, a lot more than she'd bargained for. It was sweet and it was tender. It was soft and sensuous, then hard and demanding. It brought tears to her eyes and joy to her heart.

When at last their mouths drew apart, Buck's lips moved softly against her cheek, forming the words that gave full meaning to her life. ''I love you so much, darlin'. Please, will you marry me?''

''Yes,'' she whispered, nodding her head for emphasis. For an instant there was only silence. ''Didn't you hear me? I said yes.''

''I was waiting for the *but*,'' he said with a chuckle, squeezing her so hard she could barely breathe.

Her fingers freed the buttons on his shirt, then skimmed along the sun-warmed skin at the top of his jeans. Lifting her T-shirt, his hands skimmed upward until his fingers brushed the sides of her breasts. A soft breeze kissed the bare part of her back as her eyes focused on his mouth. ''This is working pretty well,'' she said in a soft, low voice.

''Will the cats be all right for about an hour?'' he asked, scooping her up and into his arms.

''Yes,'' she murmured, pressing her cheek against his.

"Do you want a big wedding with all the trimmings?" He was making long strides toward the front door.

"Yes." She brushed a kiss behind his ear.

"Could we call Lizbeth a little later, after we decide on living arrangements for Charlie and Brigette?"

"Yes." She trailed her fingers down his chest until she touched the top button of his jeans, then popped it open.

"Are you still on the pill?"

"Umhmmm."

"Then how do you expect me to get you pregnant?"

The sound of laughter made its way from her throat. "If you've forgotten how, I'll be all too happy to refresh your memory." How could he carry her, ask questions, and still do magic things with his hands, all at the same time?

"Do you think we'll make it to the bedroom?"

Her soft laughter lingered on the summer air and wafted down the hallway to the big bed beneath their pleasure dome. Buck lowered her onto the bed.

"Love is forever. You know that, don't you, darlin'?"

"Oh, yes. Yes, I know that. Forever and ever."